Love is a Gamble:

Play to Win

A Novel
By

MELISSA
LAWSON

MOTHER PEARL
PUBLISHING
MORTON, PA

Published by: Mother Pearl Publishing, Morton, PA
www.motherpearlpublishing.com
Edited by: Shanee Garner-Nelson
Cover photos: Bigstockphoto
Cover design by: Kari Ayasha of Cover to Cover Designs
Book design by: Melissa Lawson

Ordering Information:
Quantity sales. Special discounts are available on quantity purchases by
corporations, associations, book clubs and others. For details, contact the
publisher at sales@motherpearlpublishing.com.

Printed in the United States of America

First Printing: October 2016

ISBN - 978-0-9963564-2-8

Dedication

I want to dedicate this book to "KARMA."

"Before you begin on a journey of revenge, dig two graves."

~ Proverb

Acknowledgement

First and foremost, I would like to thank GOD for giving me the gift of creative writing. I appreciate all of the many readers that fell in love with the story. Thank you to the book clubs, sorors of Delta Sigma Theta Sorority, Inc., NCCU Eagles family and many other organizations that hosted me on a book talk and supported *Two of Hearts*. I can't wait to do it again with *Love is a Gamble*. Thank you all for reaching out to me, nagging me about writing a sequel and pushing me to deliver.

To my love Bertram Lawson II, who has again supported this project and offered me perspective, guidance, and direction throughout the writing process. He has been such an inspiration and allowed me a creative space, even on our vacation.

I'd like to thank my focus group of readers this time around who helped to keep me on task and give me awesome feedback and threatened me when the story ended. Ashley Stinson, Leah Booker, Christian Wynne, Robin Torrence, and Zakia Moore, I truly thank you from the bottom of my heart for your participation, suggestions and direction as a reader and true fan of the Two of Hearts series.

To my editor Shanee Garner-Nelson, keep being you and keeping Kyla in check. Without you, Kyla is liable to say or do anything.

To my readers, I hope that you will enjoy taking another wild ride with Kyla, Vince and Sal. Thank you for adding my books to your collection and don't forget to tell a friend.

Prologue

Today, Kyla and Vince's marriage reached hit rock bottom. Their marriage had survived her career obsession, her aversion to having children and a car accident that almost took her husband Vince's life. But today was worse than all of that combined. Her biggest fear had become a reality when she walked into their bedroom and saw those letters and those photos covering their bed. Kyla stood there holding her daughter, Melanie, tightly as tears rolled silently down her cheeks onto Melanie's dark curly locks. Her heart had been ripped out of her chest and trampled on. She walked over to Vince, sitting in the chair breathing so heavily that she became afraid. He sat with his face in the palms of his hands refusing to look up at her. As her heart raced, she placed Melanie onto the floor and slowly got down on her knees in front of him. Kyla placed her arms around him and tried to lift his face up but he was solidly resistant. Despite his resistance, she proceeded to talk to him, in a calm but pleading voice hoping that he would see her as his wife.

"Baby, please let me explain" Kyla whispered through tears.

He pushed her arms away roughly and spoke through clenched teeth, "What is there to explain? These letters and pictures have told me everything that I need to know about what you have been up to in this marriage."

"I know it looks like I wasn't faithful to you, but I *was*, you have to believe me."

"You call going to Vegas and having sex with another man being faithful! You call getting pregnant by this man and inviting him to our wedding being faithful. Why the hell did we even *get* married? Did you ever love me or was this all just a game to you because I was your *safe* choice?" Vince quizzed angrily.

"Yes we were in Vegas together, but that was before we were married. I wasn't trying to be unfaithful but it just happened."

"Before we were married, huh? That's your story? We were engaged and *planning* to be married. Cheating and getting pregnant doesn't just happen so kill that bullshit."

"Okay, I know it sounds like that from the letters but that is not what happened. No, I wasn't honest with you about who he was at the wedding but it wasn't the right time to talk about it. He came there on his own and I was just as shocked to see him as you were."

"Well, when was the right time? Oh, I know, NEVER. You were just going to let me go through life thinking that Melanie was my daughter while you kept fucking with her *real* father and bringing home more illegitimate babies to me because I was the fool to fall for your shit."

"He is *not* Melanie's father, YOU ARE and I never slept with him after we were in Vegas. The pregnancy he referred to was when I was a teenager!" Kyla exclaimed.

Things were escalating and if they didn't find a way to bring it back, Kyla felt it could get out of control and, for the first time ever, even physical. The tension in the room was thick. Vince was filled with rage. And Kyla was remorseful but coming across as defensive.

"You expect me to believe that shit, with all of the lies you've been telling! So you lied to me about ever being pregnant in the doctor's office with a straight face. What was the point of that lie if you were a teenager? You know what, don't bother explaining it because I won't believe it anyway. What I *do* know is that this dude is not still sitting around professing his deep love for you if it's not being reciprocated in some way."

"It's true. I don't love him and we've been over for years. Our history is complicated and I didn't think you would understand it so I never talked about him. All that is important is that I made my choice and I chose you."

"I'm glad to hear that you *chose* me but what's fucked up is that I had to be a part of a "choice" *after* I put a ring on your finger and you said yes. Now, I understand why you were dragging your feet to get married in the first place. A wedding would just complicate things for the two of you," Vince said as he stood up.

Kyla stood up and began to stare into space. Vince was absolutely right about her rationale for delaying the wedding. Hell, Vince was right about a lot and she was running out of excuses and pleas. He went inside of the closet and came out with a jacket and grabbed for his keys and wallet on the nightstand.

"Where are you going? We're not done," Kyla questioned.

"Oh, *I'm* done with this conversation *and* you, so be gone when I get back," Vince said matter-of-factly.

"Where am I supposed to go?"

"That's not my concern. Maybe you can go to your boyfriend's house. I'm sure he'll be there with open arms," Vince said on his way down the staircase.

Kyla followed him to the top of the stairs and yelled as he went down, "Vince...don't do this, I love you!"

Vince yelled back up at her, "No you don't and I want a DNA test," as he walked out and slammed the door.

Kyla's whole world shattered when that door slammed and now she was left there to pick up the pieces. She had too many things to consider. What was she going to do? Where was she going to go? Should she stay here and fight for her marriage or just leave? She knew that he was too angry for them to even have a rational conversation so she gathered her things to give him some space. She packed a bag for herself and the baby who had been crawling around the room while they argued—completely oblivious to how the world was changing. As Kyla threw things into the bag, she decided it wasn't going to end like this. She would fight for her marriage. She would make him see that, although she made a terrible mistake when they were engaged, he should forgive her. Still, she needed to talk to someone to process all of this. She grabbed her bags, put Melanie in the car and backed out of the driveway. Just then, the thunder and lightning started. With each crash of thunder, she felt a punch in her chest; each lightning bolt felt like a pierce through her heart.

Chapter 1

Vince felt like he had been driving for an eternity while thinking about how quickly his marriage had unraveled. They were in such a good place after his car accident. He felt so sure that they were moving in the right direction until that shoebox fell out of the closet exposing all of his wife's lies and transgressions. He poured everything he had emotionally into this marriage and loved her so much. Like so many others, he never thought that his marriage could fail until that box. After an hour, Vince reached his destination and pulled into the driveway. He was hoping that his best friend and best man Jason would be home since he didn't even bother to call ahead. He got out of the car and walked up the steps to the massive brick house and rang the doorbell. After his second try, Jason's beautiful wife came to the door.

"Hey Vince," the tall, slender, but curvaceous woman said.

"Hey Michelle, is Jason home?" Vince questioned, clearly agitated.

"Yeah, he's down in his man cave; you know the way."

"Thanks."

Vince navigated through a few rooms in the house until he got to the kitchen and went downstairs into the basement where Jason was sitting in a recliner with his feet up, remote in hand. The television was blasting ESPN and Jason didn't hear Vince arrive. When Vince got close enough for Jason to notice, Jason yelled out, "Yoooo," as he hopped up from the recliner to pull him in for a man hug. They had been friends since elementary school and this greeting was customary. Vince could be vulnerable with Jason and could tell him the truth.

"Man, what are you doing all the way out here?" Jason asked.

"I needed to clear my head so I just started driving and the next thing I knew, I was all the way in Delaware and decided to come through," Vince responded.

"That's a long ass drive to clear your head. What's up with you, bro? Everything good?"

"Nah, it's not looking good over here bro."

"What going on?"

Vince inhaled and let out a deep breath and responded, "I caught Kyla cheating on me and shit."

Jason's eyes widened as he sat back in his recliner; his hands forming a steeple under his chin, "You lying man. She was fucking another man in your house?"

"No, but damn near as far as I'm concerned. I was cleaning up in her closet and a shoebox fell out with all of these pictures, cards and letters from that dude who came up to me at the wedding that she "claimed" was her childhood friend. I read through some of it and the shit he was saying was so out of order that I just snapped."

"What did you do?"

"I laid it all out on the bed and waited for her to come home so she could see what I found."

"Damn, I'm sorry man. I don't know what I would do if I caught Michelle cheating on me. Seriously I think I might go out in handcuffs or something."

"I knew I wasn't gonna put my hands on her, but I really thought about choking the hell out of her for a split second. I just left the house as calmly as I could and told her to be gone when I get back."

"So you put your wife and baby out?"

"I don't even know if that's my baby?"

"What?"

"Yeah man, dude was saying some shit about him not being able to see his baby grow up or whatever."

"Get the fuck out of here!"

"I asked her for a DNA test."

"I don't blame you!"

"So what are you gonna do?"

"I'm seriously considering a divorce. I know it seems like I'm jumping the gun but too much has happened between us for me to even move forward. I'mma sleep on it but I doubt I can go back to somebody who has lied and cheated for years. She must think I have "sucker" written across my forehead, but I'm not *that* dude. Before I met her, I had more women than I could stand. She was acting like she did me a favor by marrying me but I'm about to do her ass a favor and free her up for that dude."

"I know a good lawyer. He is one of the best divorce lawyers around. Hold on, let me go and get his card," Jason said as he got up to go inside of the office in his man cave.

As Vince sat there waiting for Jason to come back he looked around the room to take the scenery in. He noticed pictures of Jason, Michelle and the kids on the walls and they looked so happy. He could smell the food that Michelle cooked in the kitchen and thought about how he was about to lose all of this. He worked so hard; all he wanted was a family of his own and Kyla ruined all of it. Jason returned with the card and Vince snapped out of his quiet contemplation.

"Here man," Jason said as he handed Vince the business card.

"Spencer Davis," Vince said as he read the card allowed and nodding his head.

"Yeah he's one of my frat brothers so be sure and tell him "Big Dog" sent you."

"I'm not referring to you as no damn "Big Dog" man," Vince said laughing as he stood up.

"You out man?"

"Yeah I'm gonna let you and the Mrs. get back to your evening. It is late on a weeknight."

"Okay. Keep me posted on your situation and let me know if you need anything or a place to crash for a while."

"I will," Vince said as he went upstairs to the kitchen to say goodbye to Michelle.

* * *

The rain came down hard on the windshield of Kyla's SUV and she felt like every drop was representative of the tears that she felt like shedding. Melanie was sound asleep from the car ride as Kyla drove to the Mount Airy section of Philadelphia. Kyla pulled up to the house and parked the car but didn't want to take Melanie out in the rain if there was no answer at the door. She left the car running, locked the door and opened a massive umbrella as she walked up the steps to ring the doorbell. As she rang the bell, she kept her eyes on the parked car. She rang it a few more times with no answer but just as she turned to go back down the steps the door swung open.

"Kyla? What are you doing here?" Sal asked standing shirtless in a pair of red basketball shorts.

"Can I come in?" Kyla asked, almost pleading as she observed his caramel rock hard abs.

"Ummm, I...I don't think that's a good idea. What's wrong?" Sal asked as he stepped outside to get under her umbrella.

Just as she was about to tell him what was wrong, she noticed a woman walking slowly past the door wearing nothing but a white t-shirt.

"You know what, I better go, Melanie is in the car," Kyla said, feeling dejected.

Kyla started down the steps and for a split second Sal was in the rain when he realized that he had left his front door open. He could tell from Kyla's response that she saw his latest conquest inside the house. He chased her down the steps as she was getting into her car.

"Hold up," Sal said as he grabbed her arm.

"No, I'm okay. Really. I shouldn't have come here unannounced. I see you have company anyway," Kyla responded as she snatched her arm back to get inside the car.

Sal opened up the passenger side and got in and said, "Listen, she's not important. I can see that you are upset and you obviously wanted to talk to me so I'm here. Now tell me what's going on that you would drive almost an hour unannounced in a thunderstorm *with* Melanie in the car. Did he put his hands on you?"

Tears began to fall from Kyla's eyes uncontrollably. She couldn't get herself together to talk. Sal reached over and wiped each tear. He had not touched her in years and this wasn't the moment for her to get excited about it but it was a welcome feeling.

After a few moments of silence, she said, "Vince put me and Melanie out."

"What do you mean he put y'all out?" Sal questioned angrily.

"He was home cleaning up and went into my closet and found a bunch of stuff that I kept in a shoebox."

"So why did he put you out for that?"

11

"It was all stuff that *you* had given me over the years including the letters that you wrote and cards you sent recently. He knows EVERYTHING."

"Damn baby girl, why did you keep all of that shit at your crib?"

"Really?"

"I'm not trying to sound insensitive but the stuff in those letters and cards would be a problem for any man who found out that way."

"I thought I was coming here to get support, not for you to take his side when half of this is *your* fault."

"Baby girl I didn't make you do anything that you didn't *want* to—you were a willing participant and I definitely didn't tell you to keep all of that stuff in your house. Does he know that we've been over for quite a while?"

"I tried to explain that to him but he only heard what he wanted to hear and he decided that Melanie was *your* baby."

"*My* baby? What would give him that idea? I haven't touched you in over two years."

"Whatever you wrote in one of those letters about the baby we lost when we were teenagers."

"We didn't lose the baby, you got rid of it without telling me but that's beside the point. He is reaching. Do you want me to go over there and holler at him?"

"NO! That's the last thing I need is you trying to fix this. I will deal with this."

"So then what do you want from me?"

"I don't really know what I want or what I expected from you. You are really the last person that I should be running off to but I'm here doing exactly what got me in this position in the first place."

"If we're being honest, that is really your problem. You don't know what you want and I can't figure it out for you."

"I need to go."

"Where are you going to go?"

"Let me worry about that," Kyla said as she reached across his lap to open the door for him to exit her car."

Sal got out of the car and went back up the steps and watched Kyla pull off. In that moment he thought this was his second chance to be with her. It may have been under unfortunate circumstances for Kyla but perhaps this *was* for the best. Were the stars really aligning for them to be together? How could he help her pick up the pieces? Or was it already too late for them? As Kyla drove down the street she saw a message from Sal. The message read, *"I'm always here for you baby girl if you need me. You know I got your back even though it might not have felt like that a few minutes ago."*

* * *

Kyla drove another hour to her parents' house and Melanie was cranky because it was late and she was hungry. She took Melanie and her bags out of the car and used her key to enter the house. Once her father heard the door chime he ran over to the door to see who was coming in the house.

She looked at him and said, "It's me and Melanie dad."

"Hey baby, what are you doing here?" her dad asked.

"Vince and I had a fight and I just came over here to cool off."

"A fight! He better not have put his hands on you. What happened?"

"I don't feel like talking about it. I'm tired dad. Where is mom?"

"She's upstairs but you don't get to come in here talking about a fight but not tell me about it."

Irritated Kyla responded, "I'm okay dad. We can talk about it tomorrow, when I feel like it."

Kyla went upstairs to find her mother lying in bed watching television. She silently put Melanie on the bed and watched her crawl up into her mom's waiting arms. The proud grandmother was happy to see her grandbaby but was confused all the same time about their visit so late on a weeknight. She tried to wait for Kyla to say something, anything but she didn't speak, not even a hello.

"Aren't you going to say hello to your mother?"

"Hey mom," Kyla answered in an irritated tone.

"What's the matter sweetheart?"

"Nothing, I'm okay. I just want to go get Melanie something to eat."

"It's kind of late for this baby to just be eating. Why haven't you fed her already at home?"

"I haven't been home for a few hours."

"Where have you been that you couldn't feed your child?"

"What is this? Judge Kyla day!" Kyla yelled out.

"I don't know what your problem is but it's certainly not with me and you're not going to come in here yelling at me so you better pull it together."

"Sorry mom, I'm just frustrated and I don't want to talk about it," Kyla said as she left the room to heat up Melanie's baby food and bottle.

Once Kyla reached the kitchen, both of her parents showed up looking for answers. Mrs. Carter put Melanie in the Minnie Mouse high chair that sat off in the corner. Kyla tried to ignore her parents who had rolled up on her like the cavalry ready to strike. She pulled up a chair in front of Melanie and began feeding her a warmed jar of baby food. She played airplane with the spoon, made jokes and tried to drag out the feeding in the hopes that her parents would simply disappear but they were relentless. They just stood and watched. Finally, she turned to address them.

"Why are you two standing there staring at me in silence?" Kyla said sarcastically.

"Because it's clear that you have lost your mind," Her mother responded in a Claire Huxtable tone.

"Why have I lost my mind?"

"Because you came in here talking about you've been in a fight and then run upstairs when I try to talk to you about it and it seems that you have gotten beside yourself with your mother when you got up there. What the hell is going on with you?" Kyla's dad questioned.

"A fight!" her mom exclaimed.

"It's nothing mom."

"What do mean nothing? You are standing in our kitchen at nearly ten o'clock on a work day with your baby in tow and your husband nowhere in sight," her dad responded.

"Where is Vincent?" her mom questioned?

Kyla began crying uncontrollably and ran out of the room into the family room, flopping onto the couch and placing her head down between her knees. Her dad grabbed the phone to call Vince to see what happened because Kyla just wouldn't talk and before he could dial the number Kyla yelled out, "I messed up!"

Her mom sat down next to her and rubbed her back to console her and said, "Whatever you did baby, it couldn't have been that bad."

Through a nasal voice Kyla responded, "I cheated on him and he found out."

The air left the room as both of her parents searched for their next words. They looked at each other as if each was encouraging the other to speak first. Finally, her mom spoke, "Oh baby, why would you go outside of your marriage?"

"I didn't go outside of the marriage. It happened before we got married and he is just finding out and now he thinks that Melanie isn't his baby and wants a DNA test."

"Why would he think that Melanie isn't his baby if that happened before the marriage?" Her mom asked curiously.

"It was something he read in one of Sal's letters."

"Sal!" Her dad yelled out.

"What does he have to do with this?" Her mom questioned.

"That's who I was cheating with."

"Why the hell would you jeopardize your relationship with a good man for some damn Sal?" Her dad yelled.

"See daddy, I knew you would never understand our relationship, that's why I never told you."

"Told me what?"

"That I had been dating Sal since we were teenagers."

"Why didn't you think that you could tell me that?"

"Because I didn't think that you liked him or even thought he was good enough for me."

"I never disliked him but I definitely never thought of him as husband material."

"I just want to know why Vince would be denying my grandbaby if you were not sleeping with Sal when you got married?" Her mother interjected.

"Oh mom, don't make me talk about this," Kyla said as she began to cry again.

"You are already talking about it."

"It's a little more complicated."

"Well, what could be more complicated that you stepping out on your husband?" Her dad asked.

Kyla took a deep breath and said, "What Vince read was about me being pregnant by Sal when I was fourteen."

"Oh no! Do you hear this Julius?" Kyla's mom yelled through emerging tears.

"Don't be mad at me, I messed up. I was a teenager and I was scared."

"You damn right you messed up. I knew I couldn't trust that sneaky ass boy back then. I should have known he would do something like this to my little girl," her dad said.

"That was nearly twenty years ago dad and we both did it. He didn't do anything to me. It's not like he forced me to do it, I let him. We were so sheltered and couldn't do anything and for once I was doing my own thing. I had no idea that I would get pregnant."

"I guess you see how well that worked out for you, don't you! He's still ruining your life, years later." Kyla's dad yelled.

"Daddy, that's not fair."

"What's not fair is that you were running around here doing God knows what with that boy when we were working trying to give you the best life possible but you wanted to have freedom. Well, freedom costs young lady."

"Why are you lecturing me like I am a teenager again? I am a grown woman with a great career, a husband and a child!"

"Barely a husband now because of your past actions. You are failing to realize that you may be free to choose but you are not free from the consequences of your choices."

"Baby you could have come to us and we would have helped you," her mother said.

"You say that now but I didn't think that you would have been this understanding then so I did what I thought I needed to do. I went to the clinic and had an abortion without anyone knowing."

"Who paid for it?" Her mom asked.

"Alexis helped me with the money that she had been saving up from work."

"Alexis knew about this?" Her mom questioned angrily reaching for the phone.

"Mom, don't call her! I don't need any more lectures tonight. She kept my secret all of these years and I am grateful that she did."

"I'm sorry that you felt like you couldn't come to us but we are your parents and we will be here for you no matter what you think you might be going through. You are going to work this out with Vincent. You just have to show him. Go down to that DNA center tomorrow and get that test so that he knows the truth as soon as possible. Melanie needs her dad and he is a wonderful father so I know this has to be eating him up inside. Make this right with him sweetheart," her mother said.

"As a man, I'm not as optimistic as your mother that this DNA test will make this right. You have done wrong by that man and it is going to take a lot more than that to show him that you are remorseful. You have to put in some work and fight for this marriage if you want it. He has to see why he married you and that you are going to be loyal."

"How do I do that dad?"

"You're going to have to figure that out yourself."

"Okay I'm going to put Melanie to bed and sort this all out in the morning."

She got up and they all shared a group hug when her mother said, "We love you sweetheart."

"I love y'all too."

Kyla picked up a sleepy Melanie and went upstairs to her old bedroom. Once they got inside, Kyla looked around the room as she sat Melanie down on the bed to get her ready to go to sleep. This bedroom had a lot of memories in it for not just her but for her marriage. She slept here the night before her wedding. She had make-up sex with Vince in this room after their big fight and it was her sanctuary. Her parents' house gave her such peace of mind. She took off Melanie's clothes, folded them and got her dressed for bed. She laid Melanie on the bed next to her and gave her a warm bottle. She stared at her as she drifted off to sleep. Kyla checked her cell to see if Vince had called or texted but he didn't so she decided to text him.

"*Baby I messed up but I love you and I hope that you will forgive me so that we can work this out and be a family again.*" After she hit the send button she patiently waited for a response because she could see that her message had been delivered. She waited for an eternity for those three little dots on her message screen to turn into words but they never did. Instead they just disappeared. She felt crushed and cried herself silently to sleep.

The next morning, Kyla got up and took Melanie downstairs to have breakfast before calling Vince about the DNA test. His phone rang several times before going to voicemail so she left a message. "Vince, I know that you are still angry with me but I was hoping that you would meet me on Sixth Street at the DNA testing center today to get the test done. Call me back please." Her parents got themselves ready for work and checked on her before heading out.

"Good luck today, sweetheart. I'm sure he'll come around, just keep the faith," Mrs. Carter said as she leaned in for hug before going to the garage.

"Thanks mom. I will call you guys later. I love you," Kyla responded.

"I love you too."

Her dad didn't seem so pleasant but he gave her a hug and urged her to make things right as he departed. Once they were done in the kitchen with breakfast, Kyla and Melanie went upstairs to get dressed so she could plan her next move for the day. As she was getting out of the shower, she heard the text notification on her phone. She checked the message and it was from Vince. He wrote, "*Let me know where to meet you and what time.*" Her face lit up because this was their first communication in nearly twenty-four hours. She quickly responded, "*Meet me at 6th & Locust Street at noon.*" He immediately replied, "*OK.*" She was beginning to think that maybe he had come around so she texted back, "*I love you!*" She held the phone in her hand for a reply but no more messages appeared and again she felt deflated. They got dressed and headed into Center City Philadelphia to a DNA testing center that Kyla found on the internet that didn't require an appointment. She prayed that her mother was right about this test making a difference between her and Vince.

They drove around for a bit when they got into Center City and found parking on a small side street. She took Melanie out of the car, placed her into the stroller and began navigating the streets to find the test center. When she found the building, she took a deep breath and went inside. Once inside she looked around the crowded lobby at the many faces in the room and spotted Vince sitting in the corner hunched over with his head down and hands folded. She saw looks of despair, anger and anxiety on the many faces but Vince's face seemed to encompass all of those at once. This was the last place that she imaged that they would end up. She went up to the desk and signed in, took a seat next to Vince and waited to be called. As she sat down she said hello to him and he barely responded. The silence between them was deafening. She tried to work out some of her nervous energy by playing with Melanie in the stroller. Melanie began to get cranky so she reached down to take her out of the stroller and just as she unbuckled the straps, she heard a woman's voice say, "Kyla Preston, window number two". Kyla went over to the window to fill out the paperwork but Vince didn't move or even look up. He sat there frozen in his seat with a blank look on his face. The young lady behind the counter asked her several questions, which included where to send the results. She had them sent to the house that she shared with Vince. Since it was not a court involved testing, she didn't need a rush on the results and assumed she would be back home with him to receive them by the time indicated. Once she was done she went back to the waiting area to be called back. Twenty minutes passed before the technician called them back. She explained to them that the testing would be fast. They both sat down and Vince picked Melanie up and placed her in his lap. He never once made eye contact with Kyla. As the technician began swabbing the insides of each of their cheeks as he held Melanie tightly until it was over and then he put her back into her stroller. Once he strapped her in, she started screaming and reaching her tiny brown arms out for him. A tear formed in his eye at the thought of this beautiful little girl not being his. He kissed Melanie's forehead and left the room quickly to avoid talking to Kyla. Kyla chased after him, pushing the stroller through the lobby until they got outside.

"Vince!" Kyla yelled as he kept walking.

He ignored her but the sound of Melanie crying compelled him to stop and respond, "What!"

"Please talk to me!" Kyla begged.

"I really don't have anything to say at this point."

"I'm coming home so we can talk."

"Home? I don't live there anymore. I packed my stuff already and found an apartment in the city but until I move, I'll be at my parents' house."

"What do you mean you don't live there anymore?"

"I mean what I said. You can have the house for now."

"For now? What is that supposed to mean?"

"Whatever you want it to mean."

"I think you are going too far with this."

"I think *you* went too far but I am done talking about this and with you," Vince said as he walked away without even a goodbye.

"So that's it?" Kyla yelled behind him. He didn't respond.

Tears streamed down her face as she walked to the car. An elderly woman stopped her and asked, "Are you okay sweetheart?"

She wiped her face and said, "Yes ma'am, I'm okay. I just had an argument with my husband."

"Well I hope things get better for you and that beautiful baby today young lady."

"Aww, thank you."

Kyla walked to the car and began to process what Vince said about moving out. She thought about how it would feel to be alone in the home that they'd built together. Still, she was holding out hope for the two of them getting back together and the DNA test proving that she wasn't lying. Maybe twenty-four hours wasn't enough time for him to process all of this.

Chapter 2

It had been over a week since the DNA testing and Kyla woke up alone in her bed again on a Saturday morning with a crazy hangover. She lay there and pushed up the sleep mask that blocked the bright sun coming through her bedroom window. Detecting a serious headache setting in, she was slow to open her eyes. Once they were open, she looked over at the clock and saw that it was 11:15AM. Slowly, she pushed back the covers but her heart began to race when she realized that she had forgotten about Melanie. She rushed down the hallway to her room to but Melanie was gone, instantly she began to panic. Running downstairs, in and out of rooms at full sprint, she was determined to find her baby but there was no sign of her anywhere. Her heart raced, her head pounded but she had to find Melanie so she ran back upstairs to get her phone. Frantically, she dialed Vince but as she was about to press the "talk" button, she remembered that Vince picked her up from the daycare yesterday. She got herself together, and rushed through a range of emotions from laughing to crying. She pulled it together just long enough to brush her teeth and wash her face. As the water hit her face she looked at herself in the mirror and she saw a woman spiraling out of control staring back at her. She had to pull herself together for the sake of her daughter and her marriage if she was ever going to save it. The way she was carrying on over the past week, was making a case for Vince to take custody from her. Just as she went downstairs to make coffee to she heard her cell phone ringing. She turned back around to answer it praying it would be Vince calling to tell he loved her and wanted to be with her.

"Hello," Kyla said in a tired voice.

"Damn baby girl, you still asleep?" the voice on the other end said.

"No, I'm up. What's up and why are you calling me from a blocked number?"

"Oh, this is my house phone. You don't sound like yourself, is everything alright? I haven't heard from you since you left my house that night." Sal questioned.

"I'm cool, just hung over."

"Hung over? I've never known you to drink like that. Is my man still giving you problems?"

"Giving me problems? He moved out."

"Wow, shit got real huh?"

"Yeah, *too* real. He's acting like he wants a divorce."

"He filed papers?"

"No but he is definitely not taking any of my calls or even communicating with me period unless it's about Melanie."

"So he's claiming her now?"

"Not exactly, but we did take the test and I'm waiting for the results."

"You know I'm here if you need me."

"I know and you remind me of that all of the time but what does that really mean? You know what? Never mind."

"What?"

"I don't even want to get into it right now. I have too much going on right now and I hear the mailman coming so I need to go."

"So you just hang up like that?"

"Yeah, I need to go."

"Alright, call me if you need me."

"Sure," Kyla said dryly before she hit the "end" button on her phone.

She disarmed the security system and went outside to retrieve the mail. She rifled through the many envelopes until she came to the one from the DNA Center. Her heart started racing as if she didn't already know the results of the test. Once she ripped open the envelope to read the results and saw, "*the probability of paternity of the alleged father is 99.9998%*", she quit reading. She ran upstairs to get dressed with a vindicated feeling.

* * *

The sound of pots and pans being rattled in the kitchen piqued Vince's curiosity. He went into the kitchen where he found Melanie on the floor banging a wooden spoon onto a pot sitting near her grandmother's feet.

"What are you doing to grandma's pots?" Vince asked playfully.

"Oh, she's just having a good ole' time helping nana make lunch. So today is the big move huh?" Mrs. Preston responded.

"Yeah," Vince responded with a big sigh.

"Oh son, I just wish you and Kyla could work this out."

"Mom, I just need to clear my head and get my thoughts together and I can't do that in the same house with her," Vince responded as his phone started to ring.

"You must have talked her up," Vince said as he hit the "decline" button.

"Well aren't you going to answer it?"

"Nope."

"Why not? It could be an emergency."

"What emergency mom? She's been calling me like crazy for over a week trying to convince me to come home so this is no emergency and Melanie is sitting right here."

"I didn't raise you to act like this Vincent."

"Act like what?"

"Like some self-righteous person. People can make mistakes and LORD knows you've made a few."

"I'm not saying people can't but I don't have to deal with them."

"Somebody put up with your mess and forgave your mistakes."

"Yeah, but I wasn't *married* to them either when I made those mistakes."

The voicemail reminder alert went off again and he decided to listen to her message. He put the phone to his ear and listened. *"Baby, I got the test results and I want to meet you somewhere so that we can talk about it. Call me back."* His heart started racing as he slowly placed the phone down onto the marble kitchen countertop. Although he had dark skin, his face turned red and it looked as if he was going to be sick.

"Vincent, is everything okay?"

"I'm okay mom, I'll be back in a little while. Can you look after Melanie until I get back?"

"Sure honey but are you sure everything's okay."

"Yes mom," Vince said as he grabbed his phone, went upstairs to change and rushed out of the door.

Once out of the door, Vince put his headphones in his ears and started jogging to run off his feelings of confusion, worry and frustration. All that he could think about was what might be in this envelope that Kyla was holding. Could his world come crashing even further down if Melanie is not his daughter? He so desperately needed her to be his. As he jogged through the suburban streets of Delaware County watching children play in their yards, families going in and out of their homes, he thought about his past and how maybe karma had finally caught up to him. Maybe he was getting what he deserved for treating Christina the way that he did for so many years.

* * *

Vince and Christina met at Penn State University during the summer of his sophomore year. She was a young and naïve freshman who he had locked eyes with while she was moving into her residence hall for a summer program. The two began dating shortly after. As far as Christina was concerned they dated exclusively but if you ask the many women he slept with while they were together, they'd beg to differ. Christina was a biochemical engineering major from California with a good head on her shoulders. She put all of her energy and free time into her education and her relationship with Vince. Considering herself a natural beauty, she spent very little time dressing up, putting on makeup or doing much with her hair because she felt like that wasn't a priority but Vince always tried to convince her to come out of her comfort zone and every now and then she would indulge him. He was her first real boyfriend and she wanted to please him but not to the extent of compromising her morals and values, which included not having premarital sex. He accepted her for who she was, a beautiful, determined young woman who was going places; but he also accepted the countless other young women who were quick to fill the void in his sex life by giving him the panties. He was attracted to beautiful, feisty women who had an edge–but there was something special about Christina that made him want to settle down with her.

Things were going great for them until just before graduation during his senior year. They had gone to Philly for a few days so that he could interview for a junior associate position at a finance firm. It was a Friday morning and Vince was preparing for his interview. He was timing how long he had until he needed to get dressed to be in Center City by noon. His mother left breakfast for them in the kitchen before she left for work at the hospital. His two sisters had already gone off to school and his dad was at his dentistry practice. Christina was lying in the bed in the guest room looking up at the flat white paint on the ceiling. Surrounded by big white down pillows with an oversized mauve comforter pulled up to her chin, an overwhelmed feeling came over her. She had been to his parents' house plenty of times over the past two years but this time felt different for some reason. Sadness was setting in because she knew that he would be returning to Philly soon to this home without her. Vince knocked on her door to see if she was awake and she told him to come in.

"What's wrong?" Vince questioned, sounding concerned.

"Nothing." Christina responded with sadness in her voice.

"Something is wrong, I can tell."

"I just keep thinking how you're graduating in a few weeks and I don't know what that means for us."

"What do you mean?"

"I mean, you're going to be here in Philly and I'm going to be in State College. We will be hours away from each other and I won't see you like I normally do."

Vince climbed onto the bed to next to her. He framed her face with his two fingers, leaned toward her face and said, "Don't worry about the distance. I'll be up there and you can come here. Nothing has to change. You'll still be my girl."

"You make it sound so easy."

"When you love someone, you'll make it easy."

Christina's face lit up and she tilted her chin up to kiss him. The innocent kiss turned more passionate. In an instant, Vince got erect and Christina could feel it through his shorts so she pulled back.

"Let me get up and get in the shower," Vince said breathing heavily and staring at Christina like he could eat her for breakfast.

As Vince began to walk away, Christina raised the covers and said, "Don't go."

Vince turned back toward her and said, "You're not ready for what could happen if I stay."

"I think I am," she said seductively.

"Are you sure you're ready for this," Vince asked as he ran his hand over his erection.

Christina took a deep breath and said, "I am ready."

Vince pulled back the cover and undressed her slowly. He was praying that she wouldn't back out because he was at such a state of arousal that he could explode. He didn't want to do anything that would make her uncomfortable so he moved slowly and deliberately. Since this was her first time, he didn't want to hurt her and to be certain that she was ready. He caressed and kissed her breasts as she arched her back. He slid his fingers down between her legs to test the waters as he continued to circle her nipples. He stroked her clitoris slowly and she moaned loudly. He got up onto his knees and slowly removed his shorts and underwear. Once he was undressed, her eyes grew big as he reached for her hands, placing them around his manhood. She had never done anything like this before but the way that her body felt, made her question how she went two years without doing this with him. His body was chocolate and amazing. He was well endowed and she was afraid of the pain but excited all the same. He slowly parted her knees and eased himself inside of her and she jumped.

"Relax," he said softly.

"Okay," she responded, her eyes closed tightly.

He slowly pushed himself inside of her and it was tight. He had not fully entered her before she let out a scream. It was uncomfortable and a little awkward because he had never been with a virgin before so he stopped.

"Do you want me to stop?" he asked.

"No, no, I want this," she said.

He continued to push until he was all the way in and began to slowly ease in and out of her as she lay there with fear on her face until he felt her legs shaking uncontrollably. That feeling made him excited, causing him to reach his peak so he quickly pulled out to avoid any mishaps.

"What happened?" She asked quickly as she sat up to look between her legs.

"I didn't want to come in you, so I pulled out."

"I was wondering why you pulled out so quickly."

"Yeah, we don't want any babies," Vince said as he leaned down to kiss her on the forehead climbing out of the bed onto the floor.

"That's definitely not in my cards but then again, neither was having sex before marriage."

"Tina, you're in college. Who's not having sex at this age?"

"I'm not like everyone else."

"Neither am I but a brother has needs."

"I have needs too. I need a ring if I'm gonna be doing this."

Vince didn't respond to her last statement and realized that this might have been a mistake. Now she was going to be expecting him to marry her because he took her virginity.

"Let me get dressed so I can be on time for my interview."

"Okay," Christina said as she watched him walk away.

After his shower, Vince went got dressed, kissed Christina goodbye and headed out to his interview. After a few hours, he returned to the house to find his sisters and Christina talking in the family room. He overheard them talking about weddings and what type of ring Christina wanted. They didn't know he was standing there listening and after a few minutes he made his presence known by clearing his throat. They looked up and saw him standing in the doorway.

"Hey, how did it go?" Christina asked.

"It went great." Vince said.

"Do you think you got the job?"

"I think my chances are good but we'll see."

"I'll keep my fingers crossed for you."

"Thanks."

Vince went up to his bedroom, thinking about the morning and what he heard when he came home. He wasn't sure if he was ready for what she was looking for. He questioned everything he thought he knew about himself and his relationship with her. He just wanted to clear his head before going back downstairs with her. Maybe he was reading too much into things because they had just taken a big step in their relationship and he was uncertain where things would go if he did get this job. He started feeling like the walls were closing in on him as he lay across his bed.

The following week, Vince's roommate, who was in a fraternity, took him to an off-campus party at Bloomsburg University. Christina called him earlier that day and the two made plans to go to dinner after she was done studying for her finals but he completely blew her off without even calling. She called his room several times and got no answer so she decided to go over to his room and he still wasn't there. She waited for hours outside of his room, falling asleep on the chair in the sitting area within a few feet of his room. Awakened by the noise of a group laughing and talking loudly, Christina looked up to see Vince, his roommate Jeff and two girls coming straight toward her. Each of the guys had their arm around one of the girls. Once Vince noticed her, his eyes grew twice their size; he quickly removed his arm from the young lady's shoulder and walked ahead of them to try to diffuse the situation.

Christina jumped up from the chair and got into Vince's face and yelled, "What the fuck is going on Vincent?"

"Damn! She used your whole name, so you must be in trouble *Vincent*," Jeff said jokingly from a distance.

"Shut up Jeff. Tina, what are you doing here?" Vince questioned as he moved Christina further away from his door to talk more privately.

"We had plans, remember? Or did you double book?" Christina added sarcastically while looking over his shoulder trying to lock eyes with the girls walking towards his room with Jeff.

"Look, Jeff asked me to run him up to Bloomsburg and I got side tracked and ran a little late."

"A little late! It's almost two in the morning and you didn't even bother to call. And who are these hoes with you?"

"The bigger question is why are you sitting out here at two in the morning?"

"Don't try to put this on me. Answer the question Vincent!"

"What do you want me to say?"

"I want you to tell my why you stood me up and who these hoes are?"

"Why they gotta be hoes?"

"Vincent!"

"Stop yelling my name.

"Stop avoiding my question."

"Tina, why don't you go back to your room and we can talk tomorrow?"

"No! We are talking tonight."

"I'm done talking."

"You haven't said anything."

"That's because I don't have anything to say and you're quizzing at me like you're my mom or my wife so I'm cool."

"You've been avoiding me and acting funny lately so I just wanted to talk."

"Tina, I'm about to graduate in two weeks and we will be miles apart so I think we need to just end things now."

"Damn! So you're just gonna break up with me, just like that after you said that the miles between us wouldn't matter? I knew I should've never had sex with you!" Christina yelled, trying to fight back the tears.

"I never pressured you into having sex with me, you wanted to but let's face it, you made we wait for *that* for almost two years and then got all clingy on me."

"I thought we had something special so I was willing to give you something that I've never given to anyone else."

"I'm not saying that I don't appreciate the sentiment but I'm not ready to promise you forever. I'm young, about to graduate and explore the next phase of my life and not ready to be tied down."

"Tied down! Fuck you Vince! You're an asshole and don't ever speak to me again!"

Christina turned to walk away from him but deep down inside was hoping he'd run after her. He never did. Instead he watched her walk out of his life as he walked back to his room to meet the waiting legs of the young woman who he had met just hours earlier. A few weeks later he graduated and moved back home to Philly to begin working at the job he interviewed for just hours after taking Christina's virginity.

Years later, while in grad school at the University of Pennsylvania he contacted her on Facebook to offer an apology for the way that he treated her. He could see from her profile that she was doing well and lived in Delaware, working at a pharmaceutical company. She seemed happy and he thought she might be open to talking to him. She was a good girl and he treated her like shit so he wanted to make amends for his behavior. She accepted his apology and told him that even though she forgave him she had no desire to see him or have a friendship with him. All he could do was accept it and move on.

* * *

After Vince finished his run, he hopped into the shower to get dressed. After he got his clothes on, he got his phone and called Kyla. She answered on the first ring.

"Hey ba..," Kyla attempted to say before getting cut off.

"Meet me at the park near the Ford dealership on South Avenue," Vince ordered.

"Okay, I can be there in twenty minutes…"

"Alright." Vince said before he hung up abruptly.

Kyla pulled the phone away from her ear and looked at it with confusion. She was taken aback by the way he was speaking to her. Who was this Vince? She didn't know this side of him. All she knew was the loving, giving, kind, thoughtful, family-oriented man that she married; not this asshole. She got herself together, threw the results into her Louis Vuitton satchel, hopped in her red Cayenne and sped over to the park. She was a ball of nerves when she pulled up. This time she beat him there and found a bench facing the parking lot so that she could see him pulling up. She sat there, fidgeting, and inspecting every car that pulled into the lot. Once she saw his black Audi, her heart nearly leapt out of her chest as he got out of the car and began walking toward her. He was still fine and walked with a commanding presence. His face was serious, as if they were meeting to conduct a business transaction. When he got close enough for her to touch, she stood up to give him a hug and as she reached out for him, he brushed her arms away and said, "Don't bother", as he stood in front of her with his arms folded.

"Where are the results?" Vince demanded.

"Well hello to you, too," Kyla said sarcastically.

"We're not here to exchange pleasantries, so let's deal with what we came here for."

"Why are you acting like this?"

"You know why, so there is no need to remind you once again. Let's get to the bottom of this, please," Vince said, clearly growing impatient.

Kyla reached into her bag and pulled out the envelope and handed it to him. He opened it, pulled out the results and took a deep breath. He paused for a minute to read them and joy was in his eyes even as he tried to maintain a tough exterior.

Once it was confirmed that he was Melanie's father he looked Kyla straight in the eye and said, "From here on out, our only communication will be about my daughter. Are we clear?"

"Vince, come on baby, haven't I given you what you wanted? I've proven to you that Melanie is your daughter and that I wasn't cheating on you."

"Do we really need to go here again? You just managed to dodge a bullet by getting pregnant by your husband instead of by your lover. I guess you think that makes this all good?"

"I was thinking that this could at least open the door for us to talk and maybe work things out."

"Well you thought wrong and there is nothing to work out. I need to get back to my daughter," Vince said as he turned to walk back to his car without saying goodbye.

Kyla was left alone, yet again, to sit with her indiscretion. It began to sink in that her marriage may very well be over. After a few minutes staring off into the distance, she went to her car and called her best friend, Liz, to invite her out to dinner so that they could catch up. They hadn't seen each other since before the break-up because Liz was out of the country for a few weeks on business. A few hours later, they agreed to meet up. Kyla pulled up to Flemings restaurant, handed her keys to the valet and went inside. She found Liz sitting on the red leather sofa in the waiting area. Liz stood up looking stunning in black leather leggings, an off the shoulder tight shirt that showed off her amazing body along with sky-high stilettos. Kyla felt underdressed next to her.

"Hey boo," Kyla said as they greeted with a hug.

"What's up girl," Liz responded.

"Where are you going later, all glammed up?"

"Nowhere. You just never know who you might catch out here in these streets so I came prepared."

The receptionist came over to the ladies and escorted them to their seats. The server took their drink order and dropped off menus. Once they placed their order, they began to catch up.

"I see! How was France?"

"France was amazing and the French men were loving me."

"I'm not surprised; you attract men everywhere you go."

"What's going on with you and my God baby?"

"I'm a mess but Melanie is fine and getting so big," Kyla said as she pulled out her phone to show off candid pictures of Melanie.

As they were looking through photos the server returned to take their food order.

"Look at her! I need to come see her but I've been so busy these days with this merger. Has Vince gone back to work yet from the accident?" Liz questioned.

"I don't know actually," Kyla said while fighting back tears.

"What do you mean you don't know?"

"Girl, he left me."

"What! Why?"

"He found out about me and Sal."

"I told you a long time ago to leave him alone before this happened," Liz said as she sipped her wine.

"I did leave him alone but he found all of the old letters, cards and pictures that I was keeping in a shoebox in my closet."

"You were asking to get caught."

"No, really I wasn't because I was done."

"Honestly, you should have never done that to him in the first place. He is a good man who provides you with everything you need but you just had to go running back to an asshole who treated you like shit. You are a glutton for punishment."

"Damn, tell me how you *really* feel.

"I love you girl but I've been wanting to tell you this for a long time."

"I see," Kyla said as she sipped her wine.

"If I had a man like him, I wouldn't mess that up."

Feeling the conversation take a left turn, Kyla returned verbal fire, "You don't know what it's like to be with a man like him because you've never had one. All of the guys you hook up with are just as shallow as you."

"Shallow! I'm not shallow, I just don't want to be committed."

"So why are you judging me?"

"Because you're the one who was in the committed relationship."

"Look, I didn't call you for this. Let's change the subject."

The server interrupted them when he brought out their food. They sat in an uncomfortable silence over dinner. Kyla began thinking about what Liz said to her and reflected on the entire friendship at this moment. Was it selfish of her to think that Liz should have been in her corner and not judging her? Was Liz right about her? Was she selfish and self-centered? What she did know was that she wouldn't be able get to any of these answers sitting across from Liz at this moment so she flagged down their server.

"Excuse me, can I get a box to go and the check?" Kyla asked.

"Me too," Liz seconded.

They wrapped up their food, paid the check and got up from the table. They gave each other an awkward goodbye hug and went to retrieve their cars from the valet. Kyla didn't think that their friendship was over but she definitely knew that it needed some cooling off at this point. She knew that she wouldn't be able to confide in Liz without it being thrown in her face so it was best to add some distance. Once the valet brought their cars around, the two got in and parted ways, for what could be forever.

Chapter 3

It was a busy day at the office for Vince. He was in the middle of closing a big account with an overseas tech company. The late nights had been taxing him especially since he had just returned to work a little over a week ago. He had to be careful with over exertion because his lung capacity was still not at one hundred percent after the accident nearly six months ago. He was leaving the office early so he took his last meeting and informed his assistant that he would be gone for the rest of the day. Once he got down to the lobby he hailed a cab and hopped. He paid the cab driver and went inside of the big glass building to the receptionist desk.

"Good afternoon, welcome to Davis, Moore and Associates. How can I help you?"

"I'm here to see Spencer Davis."

"Your name sir?"

"Vincent Preston."

"Do you have an appointment?"

"Yes."

"Okay Mr. Preston, have a seat and he'll be right out. Would you like something to drink while you wait?"

"No, I'm okay thanks."

Vince took a seat in the mahogany leather seats and stared out of the window in disbelief. In a million years, he never imagined that he would be consulting with an attorney about a divorce because his wife was unfaithful. Being with Kyla changed him so much. He had become a shell of himself and it made him uncomfortable. Before her, he was wild and carefree but when he fell for her, he didn't want the same thing to happen with this relationship that happened to the last so he changed to prove to himself that he could be all in and now he felt stupid for going so far for her. The sound of the door opening snapped him out of his haze.

"Mr. Preston, Mr. Davis will see you now," the blonde receptionist said as she escorted him through the door to a big corner office with a picture window.

"Mr. Preston, Spencer Davis," the muscular caramel colored gentleman with a bald head and award-winning smile said as he extended his hand toward Vince.

"Vincent Preston, good to meet you," Vince responded before taking a seat.

"So you're having trouble in your marriage?"

"Unfortunately, I am," Vince said with fire in his eyes.

"Well you've come to the right place."

"I hope so because you've come highly recommended."

"Tell me what's going on."

"Lying, cheating and a lack of respect for this relationship."

"Is there community property? Children?"

"We have a house together and one child."

"Do you think this will be contested?"

"Knowing her, she will contest every aspect of this because she is an attorney."

"Ahhh, we're dealing with another attorney. This should be fun. I love a challenge."

"She is challenging but right now she is vulnerable because she doesn't want a divorce and thinks that we can work this out but I can't get past the fact that she cheated on me and had my daughter's paternity in question."

"That sounds like grounds for a divorce but before we take it there, I have an important question. Do you still love her?"

Vince paused to reflect on the question honestly and looked up at Spencer and said, "Actually, I do."

"I think you should consider mediation before going straight to divorce proceedings. Maybe this is salvageable."

"Honestly, I don't know if it is. I just don't see me being able to look at her the same after knowing what she did. At this point, I just can't stand the sight of her, her voice or anything that reminds me of her."

"It sounds like you're hurt and you need some time. In the meantime, I will gather some discovery regarding finances, community property, custody and parental responsibilities. If you are ready to fight, then so am I."

"What's the next step?"

"I'll have my paralegal get on the filing and we will be in touch in the coming days."

Vince took a deep breath and said, "Thank you."

The two men stood up to shake hand and Spencer said, "Tell my man Big Dog", I said what's up."

Vince laughed and said, "I'll let him know the next time I talk to him."

Vince exited Spencer's office and decided to go to the restroom on his way out to grab a cab. As he traveled down the hall he noticed Liz sitting at her desk talking on the phone and once she saw him, she placed the call on hold and waved to him to come inside. Once he came inside, she told the caller that she had to go. She got up and came around to the front of her desk where he was standing to give him a hug. His eyes quickly scanned her body as she was wearing a red dress that framed her beautiful body perfectly. Her makeup and hair was flawless.

"What are you doing here?" Liz questioned.

"I had a meeting." Vince responded.

"Which attorney?"

"Spencer Davis."

"Look at you! He usually doesn't take cases anymore unless they are high profile. Your firm must be big time."

"It wasn't for the firm, it was personal."

Liz looked at him with the side-eye and said, "Divorce personal."

"Something like that," Vince responded trying to keep it brief.

"I met up with Kyla for dinner a few weeks ago and she told me that you moved out."

"Yeah I did. I moved into a condo in the city."

"Where at in the city?"

"Chestnut Street."

"I live in a building on Chestnut Street."

"Looks like we're neighbors. Can I borrow some sugar?" Vince said while laughing.

"Anytime," Liz said seductively.

"I can't believe that she did me like that."

"Me either. I tried to talk to her about it back when it was going on but she didn't listen."

"You knew about this?"

"Yeah but I didn't approve of it. You're too good of a guy to be mistreated."

"Too bad *she* didn't realize that. But I'm cool though."

"Are you sure you're cool? Let me know if you need anything."

"I'm good. Let me get out of here, I have to go pick Melanie up from the daycare."

"Okay, well it was good seeing you," Liz said as she reached up for a goodbye hug, pressing her ample breasts up against him so that he could feel them."

Vince went to the bathroom before exiting the building. While in the bathroom he looked at himself in the mirror and smiled. He realized that he still had it and that women were still attracted to him, even if it was one of Kyla's friends that he had never looked at in that way. He hailed a cab back to the garage in his office building to pick up his car so that he could pick up Melanie from the daycare. Once inside of the car, he replayed Spencer's question to him over and over in his head, *"Do you still love her?"* He really needed to reconcile that with himself.

Chapter 4

S unlight was barely peeking through the blinds of Kyla's lonely bedroom when the alarm sounded at 6:15AM. Kyla was prompted to wake up and drag herself to the job that had become her outlet these days. It was Vince's week with Melanie so she had a few late client meetings to prepare for. As she got out of bed and went into the bathroom, she turned on her phone to check for any messages that she might need to answer before heading to the office. The date, Wednesday, May 13th, popped up on her phone with a list of meetings and tasks for the day but for some strange reason this date resonated with her. She couldn't wrap her mind around why. She went about her normal routine and after she put on her make-up, she reached for her jewelry and then it her like a heavy force, as she slid her wedding ring on. Today was the three-year anniversary for her engagement with Vince. It was, by far, the happiest day of her life three years ago, she couldn't have known that she would have been the reason that happiness would to turn to bitterness and anger.

As she stared at her beautiful two carat princess cut diamond ring, she wished that she could bring that day back, do it all over again, and take back all of the lies and deceit that had cost her the best man she'd ever been with. She held out hope for forgiveness and reconciliation but couldn't fight back the tears. She was growing weary from her new normal of crying, sleeping, and drinking every day. Finally pulling herself together to leave the house, she rushed to the office to make it to her first contract negotiation of the day. When she arrived at the office, the receptionist handed her papers that were dropped off for her by courier earlier that morning. Frank, her assistant, came out of his office to meet her at the front desk and reached for the papers in her hand, her briefcase, and her purse as he ushered her to the conference room.

"Girl, let me put these in your office so you can go straight to the conference room." Frank said as he rushed her down the long hallway with his hand on the small of her back.

"Thanks. I was running a little late. It was a long morning," Kyla said sighing.

"The client is here. I have your coffee already in the conference room and you need to look alive for this meeting. There's buzz about a promotion for you, which means one for me too, so you need to nail this negotiation."

"Promotion? Really?" Kyla quizzed excitedly.

"Yes! This contract is huge and if we get them to agree, you are basically a shoe in."

"I hope you're right," Kyla said as she entered the conference room.

Several people sat around the large cherry wood table waiting for Kyla's arrival.

"I apologize for my lateness but I thank you all for being here this morning," Kyla said as shook hands with everyone and took a seat between her client and Frank.

"I've given everyone a copy of the contract with the terms that we are asking for," Frank said.

"Thank you, Frank. Now if we could open to page one of the contract and turn everyone's attention to section 1.0 to discuss the terms of the "Option."

After everyone opened their booklets Kyla continued, "Due to an intense bidding war for the rights to bring Ms. Williams' book to the big screen, my client is asking Code Red Entertainment for $100,000 up front for the exclusive right to produce a film adaptation. If you skip down to section 1.1, you'll see the time frame that Code Red Entertainment will be given under this agreement to secure the funding and begin production."

Everyone began reading the agreement intensely as the attorney from Code Red began counter offering line-by-line and engaging in hard-nosed negotiations. Things were heating up but the prospect of a promotion made her fight even harder for her client. In the end, negotiations worked in her favor. She was able to get her client most of what she asked for including a percentage of the movie's box office revenues. Emerging victorious after two and a half hours, Kyla went into her office for a bit of peace. Once inside, she picked up a photo of her family and stared at it, feeling proud of what she'd accomplished today and how it would impact them. She wished that she could negotiate as well with Vince to convince him to forgive her and come home, then she would really be winning. After she snapped out of her wishful thinking, she noticed a big certified envelope on her desk with her name on it. She tore it open and her heart dropped. Instantly she was sick to her stomach when she read the document's header, "PETITION FOR DIVORCE." So many thoughts ran through her head at this very moment, *"How could he do this? Why would he do this? Don't do this."* She got up to shut her door to make a phone call but as she approached the door, one of the managing partners appeared in the doorway of her office.

"Mrs. Preston, I hear congratulations are in order on one of your biggest contract to date," Mr. Lee said with a smile.

Trying to look strong she responded, "Thank you, sir. I work for my clients and our firm and I think I've proven that I am a valuable asset."

"You are and I see big things happening in your future here. I just wanted to come by and personally tell you to keep up the hard work."

"Thanks again and if you'll excuse me, I have an important, time sensitive matter to tend to," she said as she rushed him away from her office door.

"A lawyer's job is never done."

"Never," she replied as she shut the door quickly, practically hitting him in the face.

Once she reached her large mahogany desk, she stood hunched over it like a bull ready to strike. With one hand on the desktop and the other feverishly dialing the phone, she could feel sweat collecting on her brow. She breathed heavily and angrily as the phone began to ring.

"Philadelphia Financial Group, how may I direct your call?"

"Vincent Preston, please," Kyla responded sternly.

"Certainly, may I tell him who is calling?"

"Kyla Preston."

"I'll try to get him on the line," the receptionist said as she placed the call on hold.

Kyla listened to the hold music in disgust. She just wanted it to go away and for Vince to appear, but to her dismay, the receptionist was back with, "I'm sorry, Mrs. Preston, but Mr. Preston is unavailable at the moment."

"Well, do you know when he will be available?"

"I'm sorry, I don't know but I can put you through to his voicemail and give him the message that you called."

"That's okay, I'll try his cell," Kyla responded as she hung up before the receptionist could respond.

She went into her purse and pulled out her cell and dialed Vince's number but after one ring it went straight to voicemail—he was purposely denying her call. She left a message, "Call me." She flopped down into her leather chair, put her feet up on her desk and waited one minute before her call was rejected again. She yelled into the phone, "Why are you sending my calls to voicemail?" By this time, she was too angry to control her actions and she tried one last time to reach him by phone, but this time when he ignored her call, she screamed so loud that people in the halls could hear her, "You are a coward! How could you send somebody to my job on the anniversary of our engagement with this shit and refuse to face me!" She hopped up and snatched her purse, shoved the divorce papers inside and rushed out of the office. On her way out, she stopped by Frank's office near the elevator.

"I have an emergency. I need to run out, but I'll be back," Kyla informed him.

"Is everything okay with Melanie?" Frank questioned.

"Yes, she is fine but I have to handle some urgent business. Hold all of my calls."

"Okay."

Kyla headed for the elevator and waited by the door with fire in her eyes. Once she got to the lobby, she hailed a cab and told the driver to drop her off at 21st and Arch. She rode in silence trying to figure out how not to get arrested because she knew she couldn't be responsible for her actions at this moment. She closed her eyes in quiet contemplation for the short ride.

* * *

Office buildings in Center City had good security, and almost all had the same policy to enter: see a receptionist; show your identification; and sign-in as a visitor but this one was different. There was an extra layer of security that Kyla had forgotten about. The lobby receptionist had to call up to the company to get clearance for your visit if your name was not on the list of expected visitors for the day. Suddenly, she had hit a roadblock and she had to figure out how she would get into his office without being denied in the midst of her rage. Her dreams of re-enacting the scene from *Waiting to Exhale,* where Angela Bassett bursts into a meeting, slaps her husband's secretary, and curses him out were quickly dashed. She thought about glancing at the list and picking a name but she realized that her ID wouldn't match the name so that wouldn't work. She thought quickly on her feet and went to the Post Office next door for a blank certified package in order to pose as a courier. That would get him to come down and sign for it. She returned to the building with the package and informed the receptionist that she had a delivery for Vincent Preston who works for Philadelphia Financial Group that only *he* could sign for. The receptionist called up to the office and informed Kyla that he was on his way down. As the seconds ticked away, her heart was beating so hard she felt as though people could see it about to jump out of her chest. Sweating profusely, it was obvious that her nerves were getting the best of her. As the seconds turned into minutes, the wait felt like a lifetime; she didn't have a clue what she would even say when she saw finally him. The dinging noise of a series of elevators caught her attention and she saw a dark figure in a tailored suit turn the corner. She turned her back so that he wouldn't immediately recognize her. Once he approached the reception desk to sign for the package he saw Kyla standing on the other side of the turnstile. He took a deep breath, clenched his teeth tightly and made his way through the turnstile, snatched the package out of her hand and pulled her to the side.

"What are you doing here?" Vince demanded in a quiet but commanding tone?

"You refused to answer my calls so what else was I supposed to do?" Kyla responded as she turned to face him so he could see the seriousness on her face.

"You better not be here to cause a scene," Vince said with an equally serious look on his face.

"I'm not here to cause a scene, I'm just here to get your attention," Kyla said with tears in her eyes.

"You were supposed to read over the documents that I sent you and respond to the petition."

"Well, this is me responding to your petition. Why would you send it to my work?"

"Because I knew that's the one place where you would be and you wouldn't ignore it."

"I don't deserve this Vince. Imagine how I felt opening up this divorce petition, today of all days?"

"Imagine how I felt opening up a box of letters from your other dude...and what is so special about today?"

"What? What do you mean what is so special? You proposed on this day!"

"Why is that special? You didn't even honor those vows."

"Don't do this. I don't want a divorce," Kyla said as she tried to put her arms around his waist.

"I can't help what you want. It's what's best for me and I need to move on," he said as he pushed her hands away.

"I won't sign the papers."

"That's up to you; I'm moving on. This marriage is over."

"It's not over, you're still very angry and I understand. You just need more time."

"I've taken all of the time I need and there is nothing that you can say or do that will change my mind."

"Give me thirty days to fight for you. Give me a chance and if I can't show you then I will sign."

"You've already shown me who you are, so you don't need to waste your time fighting for a marriage you never wanted to begin with. Just sign," Vince said before he proceeded to walk away.

"I am not giving up. I love you," Kyla yelled to him as he swiped his badge to go back through the turnstile, quickly disappearing into the sea of people.

Kyla stood there, crushed and feeling like the walls of the building would collapse in on her. She collected herself and headed to hail a cab to take her back to work. She said she was going to fight for him in these thirty days and she meant it. Now all she had to do was figure out how to make him love her again.

Vince returned to his office and shut the door. Something about the interaction with Kyla made him more emotional than he had at any other time since the separation. He began to question himself, his decision to file for a divorce so quickly, and the purposefully painful timing. *Was he jumping the gun? Should he give her another chance? Can he ever forgive her?* He was trying to hurt her intentionally and he could see that she was broken; he was beginning to feel unsettled with it all. She was still the mother of his child. For Melanie's sake, he didn't want Kyla to spiral out of control.

* * *

After several days of crying episodes at her desk, Kyla began to cancel client meetings and miss work because she couldn't find the will to get out of bed. She had transformed from being a driven and beautifully confident woman to a broken and depressed shell of herself. When she did get out of bed, she resorted to drinking whatever was around the house, but it didn't make her feel any better. She began to think that even alcohol hated her. Full of self-loathing, despair and blame, time was quickly ticking away on her thirty-day promise to win Vince back. And each of his rejections left her with fewer and fewer options. Faced with no plan of action loneliness and dejection were beginning to settle in.

On this particular day, she laid in bed with flashbacks of steamy hotel sex with Sal in New York and Vegas. She felt guilty recalling how much she enjoyed the way his body consumed hers. Sal made her feel good because he was the forbidden fruit and that forbidden fruit led her to rock bottom. She began to long for his touch and thought *that* would make her feel better. She fantasized about his hands on her body and his mouth making her explode. She snapped out of it only when the phone ring. Frank was calling.

"Hello," Kyla mumbled.

"Kyla, are you coming in today?" Frank asked in a concerned tone.

"No, I don't think so. What time is it?"

"It's 10:30."

"Can you cover for me again?"

"I can, but you need to pull yourself together. You're about to lose the partners' vote on this promotion."

"I know, but I can't face the world right now. I'm a failure and about to lose my marriage."

"You're not a failure, but you *are* about to lose your career if you don't snap out of it, and soon."

"I'll snap out of it if Vince comes back to me."

"That might not happen. You need to plan for your future without him."

"But I don't want a future without him, Frank," Kyla said amidst uncontrollable tears and sobbing.

"Look, let me give you the number to my therapist. She's really good and if you call her and tell her that I sent you, she might be able to get you in as soon as possible."

"Wait, you have a therapist?" Kyla questioned mid cry.

"How else do you think I stay sane dealing with your mess," Frank said laughing.

"I don't want to talk to anybody. What can she tell me that I don't already know at this point?"

"It's not about wanting to talk to somebody, it's about *needing* to talk to somebody. It sounds like you're depressed and she can help you through this. You can't just sit around doing nothing and you're spiraling out of control right now. Give it a try and if you hate it, then don't go again but you have to try."

"Text me her name and number and I'll give her a call."

46

"You promise?"

"Yeah, I promise."

"Okay, I'll tell them that you are still sick but you have to hurry back."

"Thanks Frank, I know I tell you this all of the time, but you really are a lifesaver."

"And you really are the best boss."

"I'll talk to you later."

"Okay take care," Frank said as he hung up the phone.

Kyla rolled onto her back and tried to internalize what Frank was saying. She just couldn't see how talking to a therapist was the answer and she certainly wasn't ready to face the realization of Vince not coming back. She looked back at her phone and saw Frank's therapist's name and number. She stared at the name for a few seconds and then decided to click on it. After a few rings, there was an answer, but Kyla quickly hung up. She just wasn't ready to commit. She forced herself out of bed and into the shower. Under the hot steam, she closed her eyes and went back into fantasizing; this time, Vince was her muse. He was more alluring and sensual in her fantasy than he was in real life. That was the one thing that she thought that she was missing with him. She wanted him to get inside of her head the way the Sal did and make her want him even when he wasn't around. She wanted the thought of him to send chills up her spine and give her a hunger that only *he* could feed. She loved him because he was a great man, great provider, and even a great lover, but he failed to connect with her mentally, the place where sex happens for most women. After the shower, she sat on the edge of the bed and stared out of the window, considering the merits of talking to a therapist before deciding that she was ready to make the appointment. She dialed the number again and after a few rings, she got an answer and followed through to book the appointment. As luck would have it, there was a cancellation for today at four o'clock. She took the appointment.

After sulking for hours, Kyla made it to her first visit with the therapist. She walked into the office looked around room before stopping to give her name at the desk.

"Hi, I'm Kyla Preston, and I have a four o'clock appointment with Dr. Ellis."

"Fill out this paperwork and let me have a copy of your insurance card. Once you're done, you can have a seat, she'll be right out to get you."

Kyla filled out all of the paperwork and then sat with her arms folded and began nervously shaking her knees. The receptionist gave her an occasional glance from behind the computer.

Sensing Kyla's nervousness she asked, "Would you like a glass of water?"

"No thanks," Kyla responded.

After ten minutes, a door opened and two women emerged in quiet conversation walking toward Kyla and the reception desk.

"Okay, Ms. Ford, I will see you next week. Ms. Preston?" the tall pecan-tan woman with dreadlocks said, her hand extended for a shake.

"Yes, that's me," Kyla responded extending her hand with a half-smile.

"I'm Dr. Ellis. It's nice to meet you."

"Likewise."

Once they got into the office and got settled, Kyla was immediately defensive, closing herself off from the start as she sat on the plush red couch. Dr. Ellis could tell from her body language that she had her work cut out for her. She pulled out a notepad and pen to begin jotting session notes.

"So, what brings you here today?"

"My friend thinks I'm depressed and need someone to talk to."

"What would make your friend think that?"

"I've been crying a lot, missing work and sleeping all of the time."

"What caused this sudden change in behavior?"

"My husband moved out and filed for a divorce."

"Have you been having problems?"

"Well, not exactly *during* the marriage."

"So you didn't see this coming?"

"He has been threatening to divorce me ever since he found out that I had an affair before we were married. He finally went through with it last week and it hit me like a ton of bricks."

"That's tough and I can see what you would be having a hard time with that. So basically he feels like the trust has been broken?"

"You could say that. And I don't see a way to get it back."

"When trust is broken, it can be repaired but it is a long road and going to take some work with a therapist around honesty, opening up about the relationship, and why the affair took place. Do you think he would be willing to come to a session?"

"At this point, he's not even willing to take my phone calls, so I doubt that he would come to a therapy session."

"Okay, let's take baby steps to getting him here but in the meantime we have to work on you. Let's talk about this affair."

"Okay."

"What led to the affair?"

"Honestly, it wasn't anything that I had planned or anything that Vince did to push me into another man's arms because he is an excellent husband and father. I ran into an ex-boyfriend who I had a long history with that I hadn't gotten over after Vince and I had just gotten engaged. We had unfinished business that we were hashing out and ended up sleeping together on more than one occasion."

"How long had you two been broken up before getting engaged?"

"That's the thing. We've never actually broken up in the literal sense because our relationship was more of an implied relationship."

"So if I understand you correctly, he never asked you to be his girlfriend but rather implied that you were. What was that based on?"

"We had known each other since we were kids; he was my actual boyfriend back then, but only in secret because my parents wouldn't approve."

"You were basically sneaking around to be with a man who was forbidden and that added excitement to your relationship with him."

"I guess. We were in love and I've never loved anyone that way that I loved him, and he says he feels the same."

"If you guys were so in love then why didn't you just decide to be with him openly when you became an adult and didn't have to answer to your parents?"

"Because he wasn't a safe choice; he was too unpredictable. Society expects a woman like me to be with a man like Vince because he is successful, comes from a great family, is clean cut, and isn't someone with as complicated a lifestyle as Sal."

"What was so special about him?"

"He was the first guy I'd ever been with; he made me feel special by the way he looked at me, talked to me, touched me and made love to me."

"How did he treat you?"

"Well that's another story. He lied, cheated and was sometimes unreliable."

"Is that what you think love is supposed to be like?"

"No, that's why I moved on."

"But you didn't really move on mentally, just physically. Why is that?"

"We had a bond that was complicated and I couldn't let it go. It's like he had a hold on me and we shared so many secrets."

"Are you *really* ready to move on completely? That's the only way that you and Vince will ever have a shot at repairing your relationship."

"I promise I've moved on from the romantic aspect of the relationship with Sal. Once I got married, I didn't see or talk to him again until recently."

"Okay that's a start. We've uncovered a lot today but I think we still have a long way to go. Honesty is going to be the key with our relationship as well as with you and Vince. This was a great first session and if you are willing I'd like to keep plugging away at this to help you get back on track."

"I'd like that," Kyla said as she got up.

Dr. Ellis walked Kyla to the door and they parted ways. Once Kyla got into the car, she reflected on her session with her new therapist and decided that it wasn't so bad talking things through. It made her feel better to get some of this off of her chest without being judged. She could see herself going back again. Maybe this was the start of something meaningful that could help her cope with what she was up against.

Chapter 5

A few weeks passed since Kyla and Liz had the dinner that went south. Now that Kyla was seeing a therapist, she thought it would be a good time to mend all of her relationships, starting with Liz. Kyla decided to reach out to Liz and extend the olive branch in hopes that things could go back to the way they used to be. She really needed a confidant and Liz was always her go-to person for advice and a shoulder to lean on. Despite calling a few times and leaving messages, Liz hadn't responded. Kyla was growing more skeptical about them ever getting things back on track. After pondering their relationship, Kyla decided to drive over to her sister Alexis' house to talk. When she got there, Alexis opened the door with a surprised look on her face while her children, Kennedy and Chase, ran full speed ahead into Kyla's arms with big beaming smiles. Kyla hadn't been to her sister's house since all of the drama started with Vince because she knew that Alexis would have her judgment ready so she planned to keep the conversation vague, taking special care to omit any details of her involvement with Sal.

"Hey sis, what brings you here?" Alexis asked as she gave Kyla a hug.

"I was just in the neighborhood running some errands so I thought I would stop by to see you guys," Kyla responded as she and Alexis walked into the living room to sit on the couch.

"So what you been up to?" Alexis asked with a smirk, clearly indicating that she knew what was going on already.

"What haven't I been up to?" Kyla responded with an eye roll.

"Of course, mom told me that you and Vince were having problems when she called to confront me about not telling them about your abortion."

"Oh lord, I don't know why mom and dad are taking that so hard since it was so long ago, but yeah, we are going through it right now."

"Over that?"

"That and other things. He filed for a divorce," Kyla said as tears began to fall from her eyes.

"Sis, I'm sorry to hear that. Can't the two of you find a way to work this out?"

"I'm not going to sign the papers because he's just not thinking straight, so I'm going to fight for my marriage."

"If I know anything about you, it's that you're a fighter."

"Speaking of being a fighter, I had a fight with Liz a couple of weeks ago that I can't stop thinking about. I wanted to run it by you to see what you think."

"Let me get some wine first because you already know what I think about her," Alexis said while giving her the side eye before getting up from the couch and retreating to the kitchen. Alexis returned with an opened bottle of Pinot Grigio and two glasses. She sat on the couch and handed Kyla a glass, poured the wine, and said, "Now go ahead with your story about your bitch girlfriend."

Kyla laughed and said, "Wow, you really still can't stand her, huh?"

"Nope," Alexis said as she sipped her wine.

"We went to dinner and I told her about what Vince and I were going through and how he was acting and she blamed me! She basically told me that I was a poor excuse for a wife and that, if she had a man like him, she would've never done anything to mess that up."

"She has some damn nerve talking about what she would do with a man, with her perpetually single ass."

"That's basically what I said."

"She's always been jealous of you, first of all."

"But what does she have to be jealous of?"

"The things that you have done with your career and your relationships with other people and, now that this isn't going well, she has a reason to throw it in your face."

"I don't get it because she has a great career and no, her family and love life might not be the greatest, but there is nothing about my life that she should be jealous of, especially not now."

"Girl, that's how some women are. They are in constant competition with other people when they aren't secure with themselves. I told you before, you need to keep her out of your business, especially now that you are married, because that needs to stay in-house. Your single girlfriends really can't tell you how to be a wife if they have never been one. Taking marital advice from them could be pointless, that's why I don't do it.

"Sometimes you just need somebody to talk to and confide in."

"I get that but you can't trust everybody with your information. You don't know what they might do with it."

"I think you are being a bit dramatic."

"Okay, don't be surprised when that chick is all up on your husband using the information that *you* told her."

"She might be impulsive but she ain't crazy."

"If you say so. I don't trust her."

"We might have our differences right now but she just wouldn't do that. I was hoping that you could give me some advice on how to get our friendship back on track."

"I got nothing."

"Why?"

"I don't really think she's that good of a friend, especially if she is going to kick you while you're down. Let's face it, this isn't the first time she hasn't been in your corner and it won't be the last. But you're a grown woman now and I can't protect you from people like I did when we were kids, so you have to make your own decision when it comes to Liz."

"I tried calling her a few times but she hasn't picked up or returned any of the calls so should I take that as a sign that she isn't ready to fix this."

"I would take it as a sign that she is a bitch and has always been. But yeah, she obviously doesn't want to repair the relationship so move on. You can always lean on *me* because, if you don't know anything else, I will always be there *and* keep your secrets. Before I forget, Winston has a new number in case you've been trying to call him."

"Actually, I haven't called him in a few weeks but I was thinking about him the other day."

"Baby sis, you need to call your brother. I will text you his new number. Maybe he can help you through whatever you're going through with Vince."

"He's just like dad, so I doubt he'll be of any assistance. I will call him though."

After more talking and polishing off the bottle of wine, the sisters wrapped things up and parted ways. Despite Alexis telling her to give up on her relationship with Liz, Kyla decided to give it one more try. But Liz never picked up and Kyla knew that the writing was likely on the wall.

* * *

After flipping through channels and staring at the television for nearly half of the day, Kyla grabbed her phone and scrolled through the messages. She read the transcript of messages between her and Vince that reflected a time when they were seemingly happy. She rubbed her finger across the screen of her phone, wishing she could feel him, but he was still unresponsive. Deciding to resist the urge to grab a drink and start a pity party, she did what she thought was the next best thing: she grabbed her car keys and Melanie's favorite teddy bear, and took a drive to her mother's restaurant in Northern Liberties where she picked up one of her famous soul food platters before heading to Center City. She parked her car, grabbed the bear and bag of food and went into the lobby of the loft apartments. She pressed Vince's apartment number on the silver intercom and waited for a response; after a few rings, there was an answer.

"Who is it?" the stern voice said on the other end.

"It's Kyla."

"What do you want?" Vince responded in an irritated tone.

"Can I come up? I forgot to pack Melanie's favorite bear when you picked her up last night and I don't think she can sleep without him."

"I will come down and get it."

"But I want to see Melanie and I brought food. I thought you guys might be hungry."

"I'm bringing her down too and we already ate," Vince responded as he disconnected the intercom without warning.

Kyla stood there, waiting; she was hoping that seeing her would give Vince a change of heart. She was wearing the tightest skinny jeans she could find to show off her athletic shape and a revealing top that she was hoping would entice him. He came to the door with Melanie and handed her over to Kyla but barely made eye contact as she kissed and hugged Melanie. Kyla gave Melanie her teddy bear and she gave it a big hug, then Kyla told her that she loved her and handed her back to Vince.

"Can we talk?" Kyla asked.

"About?" Vince responded.

"Us."

"What about us?"

"Don't you think that this has gone on long enough?"

"What? This marriage?"

"You know that's not what I'm talking about. This separation."

"We're not just separated. I was clear on my intentions but, somehow, you seem to be confused."

"I'm not confused. I want you back home with me. I miss you, I miss *us*."

Vince took a long hard pause and a deep breath before responding, "There is no more us and no more discussion."

"So that's it, you're really just going to end the conversation like this? Why are you being so difficult? Why do you hate me so much? Every time we see each other, you go out of your way to avoid talking to me or even looking at me. We can get past this if you would just talk to me."

As Vince turned to walk back in the building he said, "Kyla, I don't hate you, I love you as Melanie's mother but I hate what you did to this marriage and how you made me feel as a man. You cheated on me and I just don't think I can forgive you for that."

"But...," Kyla couldn't even get the sentence out before Vince disappeared behind a locked glass door and cutting off any more conversation between them. She stood feeling dejected again. She went back to her car and sat there staring off into space. She watched the people passing by in the moonlight. She watched the couples happily holding hands and laughing with each other. She wanted that again but Vince wasn't going to give it to her and he was clear about that. The longer she sat there the more the sadness crept in.

She grabbed her phone and sent a text that read, "WYD?"

"Nothing," was the immediate response.

"You want some company? I'll bring food," she replied.

"Gladly."

Kyla started her car and set off to her next destination. As she navigated the Philly streets, she began second-guessing her destination, but it was too late to turn back. She was almost there and committed to the visit. Once she arrived, she took the food out of the car and went up to the door. After the doorbell rang she was greeted with a big smile and hug.

"Damn, baby girl, you were right on time with this food. I was starving," Sal said as he let her in the house.

"I have been ducking you for the past few weeks so I thought that I would come and kick it with you for a little while," Kyla said.

"I'm glad you came through and you look damn good too," he said with a devilish grin.

"Thanks. What you up to? Why are you in the house?"

"Aaron is at my mom's house for the weekend and I didn't have any plans besides watching the NBA playoffs and chillin'. Where's your little one tonight?"

"With her dad."

"Speaking of her dad, is he still trippin?"

"Yeah, but I don't even want to talk about him," Kyla said with an eye roll.

"What are we eating?"

"Soul food from my mom's restaurant. It's two fish platters with her famous mac and cheese, collard greens and cornbread. You might have to heat it up, though, because traffic was a little crazy after I picked up the food."

"That's cool, because I know this is about to be good if your mom made it," He said as he went to the kitchen with Kyla to unpack the food. Once they got the food warmed up, they sat on the couch in front of the television to eat. The television was loud so Sal grabbed the remote and asked Kyla if she wanted him to turn it down and she agreed.

"This reminds me of the times I'd come over your house when we were teenagers," Kyla said.

"Yeah we used to pretend we were watching television every time my mom would walk in the room," Sal said laughing.

"We couldn't keep our hands and lips off of each other."

"You used to be all over *me*."

"Get out of here. That was you always having sex on the brain."

"That's human nature for men. Not a minute goes by when we aren't thinking about having sex and if we have a girl sitting next to us that lets us touch on her, we are *definitely* thinking about having sex."

"What you got to drink?"

"Alcohol?"

"That sounds good. Make me a drink but nothing brown because you know I can't handle that."

"Oh, you don't have to tell me. I know your limits," Sal said as he got up to make the two of them a drink.

She took one sip of the drink and said, "Whew, this is strong. You trying to get me drunk?"

"Not exactly. I need you to be sober to enjoy your visit."

"Remember that time I got drunk at Arnold's party and almost missed curfew."

"Yeah and I was pissed because I had to borrow a car from one of my friends to get you home on time only to find out it was stolen. That was my first time getting arrested and it was all because I was trying to protect you from getting in trouble with your strict-ass daddy."

"You know, I have always appreciated that you did that, but I was so sorry at the same time because you had to spend hours in jail and never told anyone why you were in that stolen car."

"Your family had a different expectation of you than mine did. Hell, by that time, my dad was already in jail, so it was nothing new for my family. Luckily, I was a juvenile and they let me off with probation."

"We've sacrificed a lot for each other over the years. Hell, I sacrificed my marriage for you," Kyla said as she took another drink.

"We have a bond that is stronger than most and something that most will never understand," Sal said as he got serious, put his plate down and moved closer to Kyla.

Kyla put her plate down, "Yeah, we really do."

Sal leaned over and kissed her passionately as she closed her eyes and fell into the moment. As they kissed, he slowly laid her down and ran his hand up and down her inner thighs. The alcohol was settling in, things were quickly heating up, and Kyla wanted every minute of it. She was tingling and felt his erection pressing against her pelvic bone. He slowly pulled up her shirt and began to play with her erect nipples with his tongue. With every deliberate tongue stroke, her back arched. Her body was yearning for him as she reached for his belt buckle but Sal swiped her hands away. He unzipped her jeans and slid his hand inside of her hot pink-laced underwear. He stuck his fingers deep inside of her and she let out a loud moan. He moved his fingers around her clitoris, first slowly and then faster only to slow down again as he teased her nipples. She reached for his buckle again but was rejected. He whispered in her ear, "I'll give it to you when I think you're ready for it." He wanted to tease and make her wait for it. The longer she waited the more she realized what was actually about to happen and what was at stake if she went through with it. She told Dr. Ellis that things between them were over and that she was willing to do whatever it took to fight for her marriage. This was not fighting. Sex with Sal would be giving up on her marriage and she needed to make a smart gamble. Yes, he was sexy, gorgeous and making her feel good in ways that she hadn't felt in months, but was it worth it? Once she opened up this door, she might not be able to close it. She opened up her eyes, put the palms of her hands on his chest and pushed him off of her.

"Stop," Kyla said in a whisper.

"What's wrong?" Sal questioned.

"I can't do this."

"Come on, you know you want to and I can tell by the wetness of my fingers."

"Of course I do but I *am* married and I can't do that to him," Kyla said as she sat upright on the couch.

"Since when?"

"Since I said 'I Do'."

"I can respect that, even if you are leaving me hanging like this," he said pointing to his erection.

"Sal, I'm sorry and should have never let it get this far," she said as she stood up to zip her jeans and pull down her shirt.

"Damn this dude must really be special because you have never turned me down like this before."

"You know what, he really is, and I owe it to myself to see where it goes without having *you* clouding my judgment."

"I hope it works out for you but, if not, you know where I am."

Kyla stood to walk to the door and said, "Thank you for understanding."

"You're welcome, baby girl," He responded as he walked her to the door.

"I'll text you to let you know that I made it home."

"Okay, be safe."

Sal shut the door, turned around, leaned up against the door and lightly banged the back of his head against it. He was so close to having her back under his spell. He thought it would be easy since she was vulnerable and having marital problems. Now he knew he'd have to work even harder to get her back in his arms. He didn't know what Vince had that made her want to go back to him but he was sure what he had was better.

Kyla drove home in silence without music and with the windows down to clear her head. She was proud of herself for staying strong and realizing that her marriage was worth fighting for. Now all she needed was to get Vince to realize it too. She was home in record time and texted Sal to let him know that she made it in safely before hopping in the shower. After getting out of the shower and in bed, she sent Vince a photo of herself in bed holding their wedding photo close to her heart with the caption reading, "Don't give up on us, I still believe." She didn't expect any response but she wanted him to know she was still fighting. He received the message and wanted so badly to respond but his pride wouldn't let him. He put the phone down and went to sleep.

* * *

Wrapping up another business meeting, Vince was sitting in his office when his assistant came in with an urgent message for him to pick his daughter up from the daycare and bring her to Kyla's house. Kyla couldn't get there in time. He reached for his phone to call Kyla's office, prepared to question why she waited until the last minute to call him, but he decided to just put the phone down and go and get his daughter. He was one of the last parents to arrive at the daycare. When he walked in, Melanie was playing with another boy who was only a bit older than she. Vince stood watching their interaction and thought about what it would be like to have a son. Transfixed, he didn't even realize that the boy's parent had come in and stood beside him. Vince didn't snap out of it until the boy dropped the toys and ran over yelling "auntie". Vince turned his eyes toward the woman standing next to him and was paralyzed. The child's aunt stopped him in his tracks and was one of the most beautiful women that he had ever seen. She was petite and curvaceous with straight, long sandy hair. Her smooth almond skin glowed as he looked into her hazel eyes. Vince was smitten but tried to maintain his composure by picking up Melanie to leave.

"They play well together," Vince said.

"Yes, they do," the woman responded with a smile.

"How old is your daughter?"

"She's ten months old. How about your son?"

"Oh, he's not my son, he's my nephew and he's three."

"Well he sure was excited to see you."

"I came to surprise him since he hasn't seen me in a few months."

"That was nice of you. Oh, my name is Vincent, by the way," he said as he reached his hand out for hers.

"I'm Annette. It is nice to meet you, Vincent," she said as she shook his hand.

"We better get going, I have to drop her off at her mother's house so I can get to a late client meeting," he said, trying to play it cool, even though he didn't have anything scheduled for later.

"What kind of work has you working so late?"

"I am a Senior Financial Analyst at Philadelphia Financial Group."

"Impressive," she said with a seductive smile.

"How about you?"

"I'm in communications. How about I give you my card and we can keep in touch, that's if you aren't going home to a woman after your meeting," she boldly said while handing him her business card.

"I'm going home to an empty loft apartment, so I will take you up on your offer to keep in touch; here's my card as well," he said.

"It was nice meeting you, Vincent Preston," she said as she read his business card.

"Likewise, Annette Jennings," he responded as he also read hers.

The two headed for the door and went their separate ways. Vince could not stop thinking about how stunning she was and what her legs would look like in the air. When he got to Kyla's house she wasn't home, so he used his key to get in. Vince took his suit jacket off and laid it across the bar stool in the kitchen, loosened his tie, rolled up his sleeves, and prepared dinner for Melanie since he had not heard from Kyla. After he fed her, they sat in the family room, watched television and played until he fell asleep with Melanie sleeping soundly in his arms on the couch. Around eight o'clock, Kyla came home and found the two sleeping on the couch. She grabbed Melanie from her dad's sleeping embrace, took her upstairs and laid her in the crib. She came back downstairs to where Vince was still sleeping and sat down on the couch beside him. She leaned over and kissed him sweetly on the forehead but he still didn't wake up. She figured that he must be tired so she didn't bother him. She went upstairs to get Melanie cleaned up and into her pajamas, which she slept through. Once Melanie was tucked in bed, Kyla took a quick shower, rubbed on her best smelling Laura Mercier lotion, and put on the smallest pajamas that she could find before tiptoeing back downstairs. She snuck over to the couch and straddled Vince, startling him awake. She leaned in to kiss him as his eyes got wide and he quickly got up and pushed her off of him.

"What are you doing?" Vince demanded.

"I'm kissing my husband," Kyla responded as she continued to try to kiss him. He rejected her.

"Why are you dressed like that?"

"I just got out of the shower."

"How long have I been asleep?"

"I don't know because you were asleep when I got here and that was about a half an hour ago."

"Was this the plan?"

"What plan?"

"To get me here so you could throw yourself on me? You think fucking me is all I want and will make things better?"

"No, of course not. I really had a meeting that ran late and when I saw you lying there, sleeping so peacefully, I thought about how much I wanted to feel you next to me."

"Look, I'm about to get out of here."

"You don't have to leave."

"I never planned on staying this long."

"Spend the night with me."

"Naw, I'm good. I don't know who you've had in that bed."

"Nobody but you. This is your house and you can come here any time that you want."

"I don't want to be here longer than I need to be," Vince said as climbed the stairs to kiss Melanie goodbye. Kyla followed him into Melanie's room and as he leaned over to kiss Melanie in her crib, she slipped her arms around his waist, pressed her body up against his and squeezed him tightly. He placed his hands on top of hers, closed his eyes and inhaled deeply. He missed her scent, her warmth, her touch, and her femininity. He was tempted to scoop her up and whisk her away into their old bedroom and make passionate love to her but he resisted. He couldn't bring himself to that level of forgiveness, even if it was just sex. He knew that having sex with her would open up all kinds of feelings for the two of them and he just couldn't get past the visual of another man being inside of his wife. Every time he thought about forgiving her and coming home, the contents of that box wiped away any hope for them. He knew he had to get over that, but it wasn't going to happen any time soon. The wound was still too fresh. He knew he had to go so he removed his hands from on top of hers and then removed her hands from around his waist.

He turned toward the door and said, "I have to go."

"Please, just lie with me."

"I'm sorry, I just can't," was the last thing he said before he left the room and headed down the spiral staircase to the back door. After he grabbed his suit jacket from the bar stool, he opened the door but stopped to look back at Kyla. There she stood, standing with tears rolling down her face. He could see that she was hurting. He turned to her and pulled her into a tight embrace. She cried out. Watching him walk out of the house was like reliving that moment when he first left all over again. For a few moments, they stood in silence as Vince waited for her to calm down. He kissed her on the forehead and left without saying a word. When he got into his car, he felt sick to his stomach. It hurt him to see her like that, but, he was sure, the damage was done and it was time to close this chapter in his life. It was time to move forward with the divorce.

Chapter 6

The summer days grew hotter. Vince woke from a restless sleep with sweat trickling down his back. Anxiety was settling; today he was meeting with his lawyer to move forward with the divorce. He rolled onto his back, placed his hands behind his head, and stared at the vaulted ceiling contemplating his decision to permanently end his marriage. The lasting image of Kyla standing at the house and crying her eyes out rattled him. Each time he saw her in this state, he became more conflicted. Deep inside he loved her and he could see that she loved him deeply, no matter how hard he tried to convince himself that she was an awful person. He had to admit, she was keeping her promise to fight for him. He knew he wasn't making it easy for her, but respected and appreciated her willingness to fight. Even though he said that he wanted her to hurt, he was becoming emotionally drained from this tug-of-war for his heart. His hard exterior masked the fact that deep down inside, his heart was still open but becoming more hardened with each day they spent apart.

He was reminded of his love for Kyla whenever he looked at Melanie's beautiful little face, a miniature version of her mother. Still, he couldn't shake the DNA testing and the thought that Melanie could have not even have been his. He wanted to love again, love *Kyla* again, but his pride wouldn't allow him to no matter how much he waivered. He sat in bed and convinced himself that he was doing the right thing. After showering, he put on one of his best power suits signifying he was ready for business. He left his apartment and headed to his destination on foot so that he could clear his head along the way. Center City was filled with tourists and people going to work. On his way into his lawyer's office, he found himself sharing an elevator with a beautiful woman. In his line of work, he was always surrounded by beautiful women. Since marrying Kyla, they hadn't even crossed his mind. Newly separated, he was beginning to notice all that he had surrendered for his wife. The woman and Vince quietly checked each other out until the elevator reached the twelfth floor and the door opened.

Stepping out of the door, she turned to him, "You look really good in that suit."

She winked and walked away as the doors began to close when Vince motioned for them to open again, "And you look good in that dress."

Once she heard Vince's voice, she turned back seductively while biting her bottom lip, "You should call me so we can talk more about where you got that suit from."

Vince stepped off of the elevator, "We can definitely discuss. Give me your number and let me take you to dinner."

"Dinner sounds like a plan."

"Okay, gorgeous," he responded as he pulled out his phone.

After she gave him her number, Vince turned back for the elevator to head to his meeting. He looked down at his hand realizing that, since he'd shed his wedding ring, women were coming out of the woodwork. It was clear, he was beginning to exude *single and available* to every woman he passed by. Once he got into the office and checked in with the receptionist, he went to the waiting area and picked up a magazine to read. As he sat there, Liz walked by and did a double take. She walked back towards Vince.

"Hey you. Back for another meeting?" She asked.

Vince looked up to see Liz and said, "Yeah I have another meeting with my attorney."

"We should have lunch after your meeting to catch up."

"I think I could swing that."

"Okay, stop by my office on your way out."

"Cool, I can do that."

Liz walked away slowly and deliberately shaking all of her womanly assets as Vince's eyes trailed her from behind. She coyly looked back to be certain that he was watching. Again, he couldn't help but notice how sexy she was while reminding himself that she was Kyla's friend. He turned his attention back to the magazine. After a few more minutes of waiting, the receptionist came out to let him know that Mr. Davis was ready to see him. He took a deep breath and got up from his seat, pulled his suit jacket down, straightened his tie, and mouthed the words "game time" to himself. Once inside the office, they exchanged pleasantries and then got down to business.

"How's it going Mr. Preston?" Mr. Davis asked.

"It's been tough; I've been second guessing this divorce ever since the papers were served. Of course Kyla refuses to sign them. She vows to fight for the marriage like I thought she would before but I'm ready to move forward, no mediation, no questions asked," Vince responded.

"So I've taken a look at all of the declared assets and property and it seems like you two may be headed for a pretty contentious divorce if she doesn't sign the papers. Remember, we're dealing with an attorney; she's someone who knows the law."

"What happens if she doesn't sign them?"

"Unfortunately, under Pennsylvania law, we can't force her to sign them and you two will remain married. But, we have options. If she refuses, we can request arbitration to reach an agreement."

"So what you're saying is I could be stuck in a marriage that I no longer want?"

"At least until you guys have been separated for two years. We can then file a motion based on the marriage being irretrievably broken due to adultery but we will have to gather all of the hard evidence to prove it. If she denies it, we will have to fight."

Vince sat speechless for a few seconds and said, "Unbelievable."

"Well, let's just hope that she signs the papers within a timely manner so that we won't have to go that far. Let me be honest though, you also seem to be wavering between staying and leaving. Being intimate with her or giving her any reason to believe that you could make this work could complicate things within the two-year separation."

"Man, I thought that divorce would be easier than this."

"What would give you the impression that divorce was as simple as just filing the papers?"

"I don't know, I just felt like if someone wanted out, the other party would just agree to end the marriage and be done with it."

"I wish they were all easier but divorce can be a tough situation if both parties don't agree. You need to get your hands on any evidence that will support your claim of adultery."

"I only read it in letters."

"You need to get copies of those letters if possible."

"Okay, I will do what I can."

They spent some time carefully going over all of the details of finances, property and support. Vince left the meeting an hour later feeling deflated. He thought for sure that he would be able to move on the divorce quickly but he saw now that it was not likely given Kyla's state of mind. There is no way she would agree to the divorce. He knew he needed to heed Spencer's advice and avoid physical and emotional contact because that would only further exacerbate the situation. He found his way down the hall to Liz's office and she signaled that she would be right out. She grabbed her purse and went out into the hallway to meet Vince.

"Where do you want to eat?" Liz asked.

"I don't know, this is your neck of the woods," Vince responded.

"How about this Mexican restaurant down the street? They just opened and it's in walking distance."

"Sure, sounds good."

The two headed over to the restaurant and got a table for two in the center of the restaurant. They ordered appetizers, salads and a few non-alcoholic drinks. They sat in awkward silence for a few minutes until the food arrived. Vince began to question why he agreed to go to lunch with Liz. It was out of the ordinary, and it was especially odd now given that she was Kyla's best friend. He figured it would not help him cut ties with her. The last time that he was alone with Liz was years ago when they went to go look at engagement rings before he proposed to Kyla. She didn't make him uncomfortable but there had been several interactions between them over the years that gave him pause. She had a tendency to be overly flirtatious with him but he always brushed it off because he didn't think that she would do anything to jeopardize her friendship with Kyla. They finally broke their silence with a bit of small talk.

"So what's been up with you since the last time we talked?" Liz casually asked.

"Work, Melanie, divorce. You know, the usual," Vince said laughing.

"That's not exactly the *usual*."

"It's *my* usual these days."

"I've been busy with these crazy insurance cases. I haven't had much time for anything else."

"You actually let something slow you down? That's not like you."

"Is that what you think of me? You think I'm some wild, out-of-control woman with no restraint?" Liz questioned as she dropped her fork on the floor and slowly leaning over to pick it up as her voluptuous breasts peeked out from the top of her dress.

Trying to look away and not acknowledge what she was doing, Vince responded, "I'm not saying that, but you definitely like to live on the wild side, you know, a free spirit so-to-speak; but I'm not saying that that's a bad thing."

"Actually, I'm trying to work my way up the legal ladder, so I figured I would get on my grind and put more billable hours in. Besides, I don't have a man to go home to," Liz said with inviting eyes, slowly licking the spoon.

"The only woman I have to go home to these days is Melanie when she comes over, which has been a lot lately."

Liz reached over and ran her index finger playfully across the top of Vince's hand and said, "A man like you should never have to sleep alone."

Vince cleared his throat. Trying to change the subject, he moved his hands and asked, "When is the last time you spoke to Kyla?"

"I haven't spoken to Kyla in a while but she has left me a few messages."

"Why haven't you called her back?"

"I'm just not ready to talk to her right now."

"You're her best friend and this isn't the first time you two had a disagreement. I'm sure that you can work it out."

"I'm not sure that we can work this one out. Why won't *you* work it out with her?"

"That's a different story and I don't really want to get into it."

"I want you to know that I'm here for you if you need to talk."

"Thanks, but I don't know if that's a good idea."

Feeling rejected, Liz looked at her watch and said, "I better get back to the office."

"Yeah, me too," Vince responded as he motioned for the server for the check.

Once the server dropped off the check, Liz offered to pay for the bill since she invited him to lunch. She quickly hurried out of the door, barely saying goodbye. Before Vince could get her attention, she was out of sight and had forgotten her credit card. He put the card in his jacket pocket and hailed a cab to head back to the office. Once he had gotten back to his office his assistant notified him of a delivery that had just come for him. It was fruit basket that had come from Kyla. The card read, "Love conquers all". He sat down in his chair and read it over and over before picking up the phone.

"Can you take this arrangement to the break room for the staff?"

"Sure thing Mr. Preston," his assistant responded as he ripped the card and threw it in the trash. That was his first step to emotionally detaching. With each rip of the card his heart grew harder. He exhaled as each piece of paper fell into the trash. By day's end, he peeked into the break room and noticed that all of the fruit and chocolate was gone and he exhaled with a tiny bit of peace.

* * *

Vince had a long day at work after his strange lunch with Liz and the delivery from Kyla. He got in, took off his clothes and lay across the couch to watch television. His phone began to buzz when he noticed a text message from Kyla. He clicked on it and saw a picture of Melanie and Kyla with a caption that read, "Did you like our gift?" He wanted to respond to

Melanie but he knew that was impossible since she was only ten months old and couldn't actually read so it would be responding to Kyla. He ignored the message. Just as he settled in he got a call from a blocked number. He wanted to let it ring because he assumed it was Kyla calling. After the third ring, he sat up on the couch and answered the phone.

"Hello," Vince says.

"Hi, may I speak to Vincent?"

"This is Vincent."

"Hi, this is Annette."

Suddenly his eyes lit up and with a smile he asked, "What's going on, Annette?"

"I just got back into town and thought that I would give you a call."

"I'm glad that you called me. I was beginning to think that you forgot about me."

"How could I forget about you? You had such a memorable smile and such beautiful skin."

"I see you're not shy and I like that. So tell me about yourself, Ms. Jenkins?"

"What do you want to know?"

"Whatever you want me to know."

"I'm twenty-nine and I just moved here from New York. I graduated from NYU with a communications degree five years ago and worked at a communications firm in New York but when they had an opening here in Philadelphia, I decided to transfer to be closer to my family. I'm a hopeless romantic and lover of sports. What about you? Tell me about yourself."

"I'm thirty-three, from Philly, and, as I told you before, I am a financial analyst and a dad. I love to cook, travel and do romantic things for my lady. What's a woman like you doing without a man?"

"Actually, I'm technically married but we are going through an amicable divorce. We weren't on the same page when it came to having children. I wanted children but he waited until we were married to finally admit that he didn't and I wasn't willing to wait until he changed his mind, so we parted ways."

70

"Wow, that is crazy."

"What's so crazy?"

"How similar our situations are."

"Are you married too?"

"Yeah, technically, but I filed for a divorce. She didn't want kids in the beginning but eventually she came around and we had our daughter but then I found out she was cheating on me."

"Damn, I know that was hard. You seem like a great guy."

"I am but she didn't appreciate me."

"Who was she cheating with?"

"I really don't want to talk about her so let's talk about you. What do you like to do for fun?" He asked as he changed the subject. The two talked for what seemed like hours. He felt so comfortable talking to her and they had so much in common. He wanted to know more and could see himself talking to her again and taking her out. There was something alluring and sexy about her, even over the phone, and he found himself smitten like a schoolboy all over again. He was so self-assured and confident and didn't hold anything back. He hadn't had this much of a conversation with a woman since Kyla. Annette was turning out to be a breath of fresh air. In many ways, she and Kyla were a lot alike but he didn't know if that was a good or bad thing. He was willing to take the chance to find out.

Chapter 7

Several days passed after Kyla had her emotional breakdown in Vince's arms. Seeing Vince walk out of the door broke Kyla all over again. She tried texting, calling, and sending gifts but he was still non-responsive. The end seemed near and inevitable and it killed her to know that there was nothing she could do about it. She decided to contact Dr. Ellis for help. On her way to the office, she gave Vince's job one last call but his assistant insisted that he was going to be unavailable all day. After checking in, Dr. Ellis immediately called Kyla back to her office. Once she sat on the couch to start their session, Dr. Ellis noticed the sweat beads forming on Kyla's forehead. Dr. Ellis offered her water but she declined.

"So how have things been going since the last time we spoke Ms. Kyla?" Dr. Ellis questioned.

Kyla's bottom lip began to tremble as she stared right through Dr. Ellis before breaking down into tears, finally answering, "Not good, not good at all."

Dr. Ellis handed her a box of tissues and said, "It's okay, let it out and we can talk when you're ready."

Kyla dabbed her eyes with a tissue a few times, blew her nose with another and balled them up in her hands before responding, "it's really over" as more tears fell.

"What's really over?"

"The marriage. I tried to build trust like you said, but it just didn't work, and he won't take me back, no matter what I do."

"Let's talk about the trust building steps that you took."

"I called consistently, texted, sent gifts but he didn't respond to any of it."

"Okay, those are all everyday activities, none of which will actually get his attention because he expects you to call and text at this point because you two have a daughter together so that type of communication is necessary. I'm also concerned about the frequency and level to which you are trying to force him to communicate with you because that can be unhealthy for both of you."

"I don't know any other way to get his attention. What else is there?"

"There are less aggressive ways. You want to let him know how you feel and to be as honest as possible like we spoke about in our last session. Show him that you are willing to confront the situation head-on and take full responsibility for what you've done. Yes, you've said, 'I'm sorry.' Yes, you've admitted to having an affair but, because he has shut you out, you haven't been able to tell him the truth."

"What is the truth?"

"That's for you to figure out."

"I told him that I had the affair when we were engaged, what else does he need to know?"

"That's common knowledge to him now, but it's not the truth."

"I'm afraid I don't follow."

"Why you did it and what the other guy *actually* meant to you is what he is after."

"I don't see how telling him that would accomplish anything."

"It will accomplish the trust building that you need. Deep down inside, he wants to know *why* he wasn't good enough and *why* you chose the other man over him but his ego and pride won't allow him to ask you those questions because he doesn't want to openly compare himself to this other guy. Like most men with healthy self-esteem, he likely went through life feeling as though he could satisfy any woman, which included his wife. When he couldn't it created a feeling of inadequacy within him that looking at you or hearing from further exacerbates."

"He won't talk to me long enough to have that type of dialogue."

"You can't force him to talk to you so stop trying to have a two-way dialogue and send him a letter. When you write him a letter, he'll have no choice but to sit down and listen to what you're trying to tell him. His curiosity may cause him to read it, even if he doesn't respond. In the letter, you'll need to put all of your cards on the table and gamble with the house money. At this point you really have nothing to lose. Tell him about the things you've shared with me at our last session about your feelings for the other man and why you held on to him for so long. Let him know that the affair was never about *him*, and how it was about *you*."

"How will I know that he read it?"

"You won't know it, but you will have achieved two of the steps in the trust building process, which is honesty and ownership."

"I really just want him to forgive me and drop this whole divorce."

"Kyla, that's up to him but you have to stop carrying all of this burden. Much of the hurt you are carrying is saddled with guilt and shame because you haven't been able to be honest with yourself or your husband. He has also accomplished his task of transferring his pain onto you but now you have work on forgiving yourself even if he never does."

"Since I'm being honest, I had a moment of clarity when I went to see the other guy a few weeks ago because I was feeling lonely and he wanted to be intimate with me. I told him that I needed to be with my husband and that I no longer saw him that way. That's how I knew I was really ready to be committed to Vincent, there was finally no more temptation."

"I'm glad that you've finally gained some clarity but you still have a long way to go. I would like to continue this session but we've reached our time limit. I hope you'll come back and see me soon and next time try not to wait until you've reached this level of turmoil."

"Thanks Dr. Ellis and I promise I will be back sooner than later."

Kyla got up from the couch with a sense of calm. She drove home imagining what she would say to Vince in her letter. She kept thinking about how much she was willing to disclose and how much it could cost her. Kyla wanted to see Vince's face one last time but Dr. Ellis told her to give up on forced interaction. Instead, she went on to pick Melanie up from daycare.

* * *

The Philadelphia Financial Group was unusually busy; the market was experiencing deep fluctuations resulting from international crisis and the analysts were working around the clock. After back-to-back client meetings, Vince had a minute to come up for air. He retreated to his office to clear his head. On the way in, his assistant stopped him to brief him on missed messages. She informed him that he had a missed call from Kyla, which he ignored, but he was intrigued by a message left from Annette. Finally, he made his way into his office but, as soon as he about to return Annette's call, he was called into another meeting with senior management. He walked with the older gentlemen past glass conference rooms full of people conversing and flipping through portfolios as butterflies began to form in his stomach. He couldn't help but to wonder what the meeting was about. He ran through his previous meetings in his head and considered what he might have said or done because they were both stone-faced. As they turned the corner to enter one of the firm's largest offices, sweat began to form under his collar. The oldest gray-haired gentleman took his rightful place behind the desk in the office and offered Vince and his supervisor a pair of comfortable black leather chairs facing him. Nervously, Vince gazed out of wall length glass window that perfectly showcased the Philadelphia skyline. He could see the haze in the sky from the intense heat outside, which looked eerily representative of how he was feeling inside. He stared out of the window until he heard the older gentleman begin to speak and he snapped out of it.

"Mr. Preston, busy day today, huh?" the gentleman asked.

"It's been hectic Mr. Schwartz but it's nothing that I can't handle," Vince said sternly as his supervisor nodded in agreement with a smile.

"Mr. Cohen and I have been getting some feedback from many of your clients over the past year."

"Okay," Vince said in a concerned tone.

"They really expressed accolades for your account management and how you execute with care and concern for their bottom line. They've also spoken about your management of their portfolios that have resulted in big dividends."

"Personally, I've been pleased with how you've handled some responsibilities of quite a few of our toughest and largest mergers," Mr. Cohen, his supervisor, chimed it.

"Mr. Preston, it seems that you really know your analytics and we're impressed by that," Mr. Schwartz continued.

"Thank you. I try to stay on top of current market trends and business dealings both domestically and abroad," Vince boasted.

"We are aware and it is paying off. We brought you here because we have an opening beginning on July 15th and we would like to promote you to fill the vacant position of Associate Vice President of Mergers and Acquisitions. How does that sound?"

"That sounds great," Vince said with a huge toothy smile.

"You'll be receiving a healthy salary increase, eligibility for bonuses, a travel expense account and a larger office adjacent to the conference room. You can talk to HR about any of the salary specifics."

"I really don't know what to say."

"I know you need a minute to let this all sink in but you've earned it and let me be the first to congratulate you on your promotion," Mr. Cohen said as he shook Vince's hand.

"Now you can go home and tell that beautiful wife of yours that you are going to take her on an expensive vacation this summer with this big money you're about to earn," Mr. Schwartz said followed with hearty laughter.

They had no idea that Vince was going through a divorce so while he laughed on the outside with them, he was sick deep inside. A new salary meant that there would be more for Kyla to fight for in this surely contentious divorce.

He replied with a smile, "I'll be sure to tell her sir and I bet she'll be happy to pack a bag."

He stood and shook hands with the two men and made his way back around the building to pack his briefcase. He was so excited that he didn't know who he should tell first about his promotion. He pulled out his phone and scrolled until he reached the first person he wanted to call and pressed their name. The phone rang a few times before there was an answer.

"Hello, Mr. Preston," the seductive voice said on the other end.

"Hello, Ms. Jennings. How are you today?" Vince responded playfully.

"My day is better now that you've called me."

Vince could hear her smile through the phone as he responded, "I'm glad that I could make your day with a phone call. I saw that you left me a message earlier and wanted to get back to you so you wouldn't think that I was ignoring you."

"I know you're a busy man, Mr. Preston. I was trying to see if you had plans this evening after work."

"Actually I don't but I will if you are going to be making some for me."

"I was thinking about cooking for you at my place."

"I haven't had a home-cooked meal in a minute."

"Well that's why I offered. I figured a handsome, hardworking bachelor like yourself probably doesn't have much time to spend in the kitchen whipping up gourmet meals."

"You're absolutely correct and I would love to take you up on that offer. What time should I be there and should I bring anything?"

"I will see you around 8:00 and just bring yourself and your appetite. I'll text you my address when we hang up."

"I got you covered. I'll see you at 8:00."

"See you then."

"Okay, gorgeous," were Vince's last words before hanging up the phone.

He rushed home to shower and get ready for his date with Annette. He was looking forward to celebrating his new promotion with her. On his way home, he picked up a few bottles of wine.

Kyla arrived home earlier than usual because she picked Melanie up directly after counseling. She wasted no time getting started on her letter to Vince. Since she thought about what she would say all the way home she was anxious to get started. She knew it wasn't going to be easy. After putting Melanie down in the family room with a bunch of toys, she grabbed a legal pad and a bottle of wine and put pen to paper. She wrote a few lines that didn't feel right so she tore the paper off of the pad, threw them in the trash, and started over. This happened a few times before she settled in on what the letter would be.

> *"Dear Love,*
>
> *I have decided to stop trying to reach out to you by phone or in person because none of that has worked. I've also decided to stop apologizing to you because I know it is falling on deaf ears. Instead I've decided to open my heart and tell you the truth. I've been seeing a therapist and she said that the best thing that I could do for you is to tell you the truth and let you do what you want with it. Yes, I cheated on you when we were engaged and during the first few years leading up to our engagement. I didn't do this because you weren't enough for me, in fact, you were MORE than enough for me and I was afraid to accept that. I was afraid to accept that someone else was better than what I had settled for my whole dating life. It was never my intention to make you feel inadequate in any way. I was physically and emotionally attached to another man for nearly twenty years that I was unable to move on from. He was my first love and the first guy I had ever been with sexually. He had a hold on my heart, my soul and me. I felt like I had a connection with him that I couldn't have with you or anyone else no matter how hard I tried. Once we got married, I knew I was mistaken, I connected my soul to yours the moment I said my vows to you. When I accepted your engagement ring, I had every intention of being the best fiancée that I could be but I fell short.*
>
> *At times, I was unable to give you what you needed because I was sharing my heart with someone who didn't deserve it. Every time I tried to cut him off, he sucked me back in. He knew all of my weaknesses and MOST of my secrets. The truth is, I didn't tell either of you about my first pregnancy. He didn't know that I was pregnant when I was fourteen by him. In fact, nobody knew except Alexis and me. What you read was his reaction to the fact that I never told him and his belief that I denied him the opportunity to become a father to a child that we created together. I never told you about him because I couldn't risk the chance of anyone ever finding out*

about our relationship, including you. The only other person to know the truth about my relationship with him was my cousin, his best friend Vance, who he attended our wedding with. I never invited him to our wedding. I kept my relationship with him secret from my parents. They believed we were friends and I knew they never approved of him, his lifestyle or his family's circumstances. I want you to know that I didn't choose you because you were the "safe" choice, I chose you because you chose me. You put me first and showed me what mutual love, respect, and dedication felt like. Our love was never one-sided, it was always reciprocated but I didn't understand that because I had never felt love from men besides my father and brother. I assumed he loved me, but learned later that his feelings were based on control. He wanted to be with other women and do whatever he wanted while expecting me to accept it and wait for him. So often, I was there waiting with open arms and he learned to count on that. The affair was never about sex; it was about my unhealthy emotional attachment to him. Once we got married, I fully committed to you and never saw him again. He showed up at the wedding because he never thought that he would lose his control over me. When he saw me on our wedding day, he knew he had lost and he knew it was over. We parted ways for good. I'm not making excuses for my infidelity, or for breaking your trust but I am letting you know where my heart was at the time and where it is right now. My heart is and has been right here with you and our daughter. The unfaithful part of my life is completely over and has been for some time. I hope that one day you will find it in your heart to forgive me and put our family back together. I never wanted to hurt you but I did and I am sorry. I want to earn back your trust if you find it in your heart to give me a chance. I'll be waiting for you when you're ready to come home.

  Your Wife,

  Kyla"

Before she knew it, the letter was complete and so was the bottle of wine she started. Kyla folded the letter, placed it in an envelope and decided that she was going to get her husband back by hand delivering it tonight. She strapped Melanie in her high chair and fed her dinner. After dinner, she washed and changed Melanie into fresh pajamas, and called her mother to see if she could watch Melanie for a few hours. To her relief, her mother agreed. She got dressed, threw the letter in her purse along with a Coke bottle and drove over to drop off Melanie. She made no small talk with her parents, made no mention of her destination before hurrying out of sight. Tipsy, she sped through streetlights and hopped on the expressway to make her way downtown. She finally arrived at Vince's apartment building, parked her car out front, checked her red lipstick in the rearview mirror, took a gulp from her Coke that was mixed with Jack Daniels, and fed the meter for the maximum allowed time. She had a good feeling about this letter delivery. She struggled to walk straight in her super high red pumps and overly tight snap front black dress. The dress was so tight, it looked like another layer of skin. She wanted to surprise Vince, and stood outside pretending to be on her phone while she waited for someone to exit the building before grabbing the door and going inside. As she got on the elevator she grew anxious about how the letter might impact their divorce given that she was admitting her infidelity on paper. She began to second-guess herself as the doors of the elevator opened up and she saw Vince standing on the other side as if he were waiting for the elevator to come. She stepped off and they let the door close.

"Kyla?" Vince said confused.

"Surprised to see me?" Kyla asked.

"Actually, I am."

"Where are you on your way to looking all good?"

"I could be asking you that same question but I won't," Vince said as he looked her up and down noticing her outfit.

"I came see you and drop something off."

"You could've called first."

"Call? You don't even answer any of my calls or my texts."

"So you just show up unannounced?"

"Yes, to give you this," Kyla said as she pulled the letter addressed to him out of her purse.

"What is this?"

"You'll see when you open it. Why don't we go inside so you can open it now?"

"I'm actually on my way out on a date right now."

"A date!" Kyla exclaimed.

"Keep your voice down."

"Why do you need a date when you have all of this right here in front of you," she said while rapidly unsnapping her dress and holding it open with one hand on each side to reveal the sexy red lingerie with the middle missing from the underwear.

"What the hell are you doing?" Vince said as he looked away and then snatched her by the arm towards his apartment door.

As he rushed to put the keys in the door, Kyla slid her hands down the front of the outside of his jeans, wrapped her hands firmly around his massive manhood and said, "Don't act like you still don't want to fuck me."

"Are you drunk?" he asked as he opened the door to get inside and throw the letter onto the table as she follows behind.

"Drunk in love baby," she said, slurring as she dropped her dress to the floor.

"You've got to be kidding me right now."

"No, I'm not, I want you now. I want you inside of me," Kyla said as she moved close to him and put his hands on her nearly exposed breasts and tried to kiss him.

"Stop!" he exclaimed as he removed his hands and placed them in the air. "You are making a fool of yourself," he continued as he backed away from her.

She started singing loudly, "I'm a fooooool, such a fooooool for you," trying to unbuckle his jeans.

"Why do you think randomly having sex will solve anything between us? That's what got us here in the first place...sex!"

"Noooo, this is different. It's not random, it's deliberate, and I want it," Kyla said in a silly but seductive state as she stumbled to her knees licking the front of his jeans in slow motion.

Vince was trying to resist but he was getting turned on by her naked and begging body. He hadn't been with anyone sexually since they'd broken up but he heard the voice of his lawyer saying, *"don't do it"* in the back of his mind, "Come on, get yourself together. I gotta go."

81

"So you're just going to leave me here like this," she said as she laid back onto the floor and opened her legs to expose her freshly waxed womanhood that she ran her fingers across slowly to get his attention."

Vince knew that if he was going to survive this moment of weakness, he needed to get her out as fast as possible so he reached down, pulled her up and threw the dress at her and said, "It's time for you to leave."

"But…"

"There are no buts, it's time for you to go, now put your dress on so I can leave."

Kyla stood up, put her dress back on and turned to him and said, "So, you really don't want me any more huh?"

"We're not doing this now," he said as he pulled her to the door and ushered her out.

"Will you at least read my letter?"

"I'll consider it," Vince said as he shut the door on her"

He looked down at his watch and realized how late he was running so he called Annette to tell her that he was on his way and that he had run into some traffic. She understood and ensured him that the food would be warm when he got there. He wanted to give Kyla some time to leave the area but he had no confidence that she would actually go anywhere so after about ten minutes, he went out of the back entrance, looked around to see if the coast was clear, and headed down a side street to get to the garage where his car was parked. He wanted to be sure she wasn't crazy enough to follow him, although after what he just witnessed, she might be officially insane.

Kyla sat outside of Vince's apartment in her car waiting for him to come out. She wanted to stop him from leaving for his date, if that's where he was really going. Against her therapist's orders, she tried to force herself on him again and she started feeling horrible about it. Tears began to roll down her face as she realized what she was doing and how she was only pushing him away further. She fumbled through her purse to find that Coke bottle to ease her pain. She drank the entire bottle as fast as she could and looked down at her phone and saw the beautiful face of her daughter, which made her cry even more. She sent her assistant Frank a text message asking him to come and get her because she was in no condition to drive. She told him where she was and he took a cab over there to drive her home.

* * *

Driving clear across town in record time, Vince managed to arrive at Annette's house only fifteen minutes late. He parked and walked up the steps to her beautiful twin home on a tree-lined street in the Chestnut Hill section of the city. He looked over his shoulder a few times before ringing the doorbell just to be sure Kyla was out of sight. Once he felt certain that he had not been followed, he rang the bell. Annette opened the door looking like a supermodel. She was wearing a short, skin tight halter dress that accentuated every curve and showed off her perfectly sun kissed skin.

"Welcome to my home, Mr. Preston," Annette said as she ushered him inside.

"I love it when you call me that," Vince said with a sly grin.

"I'll have to remember that," she said as she winked playfully.

"It smells good in here. I only get these kinds of smells when I visit my mom."

"Oh really, well we're going to have to change that now, won't we?"

"This is a nice place you have here," he said as he looked around.

"Thank you, it's one of my family's properties. Someone had just moved out when I came to town and I moved right in. Let me take you the grand tour," she said as she grabbed his hand and took him around the house. He made sure to take a mental note of her bedroom location for future reference.

"You hit the jackpot on this one."

"I know, it didn't need any work or anything," she said as she showed him to the living room couch.

"Lucky you. I had my last house built so that we would have everything that we wanted," he said as he sat down.

"Well, aren't you sweet," Annette said as she joined him on the couch.

"I guess you could say that I like to deliver."

"I see. Can I offer you a something to drink?"

"I'll take some water right now. I did bring you two bottles of wine, but I forgot them in the car, I can run out to go get them."

"No rush, we have plenty here," she said as she pointed to the wine rack that was stocked with bottles.

"I see you are quite the wine connoisseur."

"You could say that. I like fine things and that includes my wine. Are you ready to eat?"

Vince was just taking it all in when he responded, "Sure, I'm ready whenever you are."

Annette escorted Vince into the dining room, dimmed the lights and lit some candles. She brought the food out to the table one plate at a time for each of them and poured red wine into the two glasses that were on the table situated near the plates. He looked down at his plate draped with delicious chili ginger glazed salmon, neatly placed on a bed of chopped asparagus with a side of roasted red potatoes.

"This looks amazing," Vince commented.

"I hope it tastes that way," Annette countered.

The two talked and ate for a while and the conversation was moving with ease. They were moving past the superficial beginning stages and learning about one another on a deeper level and Vince was feeling her vibe. After they were finished with dinner, she got up from the table to clear their plates and he watched her every move and fantasized about what she would look like with that dress on the floor. He began daydreaming about Kyla with her crotchless panties lying on the floor while she pleasured herself in slow motion. When Annette appeared from the kitchen, he snapped out of it. She was carrying a plate of chocolate covered strawberries and another bottle of wine to the living room and invited him to join her. He followed carrying the empty wine glasses from the dinner table. They sat back down on the couch as she placed the plate of strawberries on the coffee table and poured the wine. She turned on love songs on Pandora by connecting her phone to a speaker dock and turned to face him on the couch.

"How was the food?" Annette asked.

"It was great. I could get used to this kind of treatment," Vince responded with a smile as he sipped his wine.

"More to come," she said as she picked up her glass to join him.

"This dinner came at the perfect time. I got a promotion today at work and I couldn't think of a better way to celebrate than with a home cooked meal."

"It looks like congratulations are in order. So what do I call you now Mr. Preston?"

"You can keep calling me Mr. Preston but add Vice President to that," he said jokingly.

The longer they talked and the more they drank, the more Vince became attracted to her physically. Still, he continued to have flashes of his naked wife. Annette reached over to grab a strawberry and offered to feed it to him and he obliged. She seductively put it up to his lips, which wasn't helping his cause and said, "For you, Mr. Vice President." Finally, after staring at her in that tight dress and her full lips he turned to her and asked, "Can I kiss you?" She whispered, "yes," and he leaned in to kiss her. They slowly explored each other's mouth. Annette climbed onto his lap and kissed him passionately. She felt him becoming aroused. He pulled down her halter dress exposing her breasts and began to caress them with both hands. Vince played with her nipples with his index fingers and tongue as she softly moaned. Once Vince could see that she was open, he slid both hands under the back of her dress and around her waist to firmly grip her while moving his tongue slowly down her neck to reach her right nipple and then the left. Annette slid her hand down Vince's jeans and once she reached his erection, her eyes got big. She became excited for what was in store. Quickly, she unzipped his pants to expose his erection and began stroking him slowly. He knew that he wouldn't last too long with her doing that so he picked her up and headed up the steps to her bedroom. Once inside he laid her down on the bed and pulled her dress over her head, leaving her with nothing but lace black underwear. He stood up and unbuckled his pants and let them fall to the floor along with his boxer briefs. She watched in anticipation as he came toward the edge of the bed still fully erect. She leaned over and took him fully into her mouth while he was still standing. He reached down and grabbed the back of her head and closed his eyes. With every in and out stroke he felt himself about to climax so he pulled back, spun her around and aggressively tore off her underwear. Still standing, he entered her from behind and began pounding away like he had just been released from prison. She yelled out, "Oh, Mr. Preston," with every stroke, which only excited him more. As he felt himself reaching his peak again, he pulled out and kneeled down to stroke her with his tongue until her knees began to shake and she exploded. At that very moment, he climbed in the bed and inserted himself again and stroked her until he pulled out quickly onto her bed to finish. They both rolled over glistening with sweat and laid in silence when a sudden guilt set in. This was the first woman he had been with in years besides his wife and he was still technically married. She could sense that something was wrong as he grew quiet

"Are you okay?" Annette asked.

"Yeah, I'm good," Vince responded.

"You are good," she said playfully trying to break the ice.

"Likewise," he said as he rolled over to go to the bathroom.

"The towels are in the linen closet."

"Thank you," Vince said as he stopped by the hallway linen closet on his way to the bathroom. Once inside, he washed up and thought about what he had just done. He was sexually satisfied but it didn't feel the same as when he made love to his wife. With the door to his marriage closed, he would have to learn to get over it. Once he returned from the bathroom, he saw Annette draped across her bed and he leaned over to kiss her.

"Can I get you anything else? A round two maybe," Annette joked.

"No, gorgeous, I am going to get out of here. I have to get home, I have a meeting in the morning and I don't want to be worn out," he said as he started putting his clothes back on.

"Let me get some clothes on so I can walk you out."

"Cool."

Annette got up and grabbed her robe to go to the bathroom to get cleaned up before walking Vince to the door. Once at the door, they kissed goodbye and parted ways.

Chapter 8

It was early Saturday morning and the past few days had been busy for Vince with work and managing the women in his life so he needed time to unwind as he would often do whenever his schedule wasn't so hectic. He headed to meet three of his childhood friends at the YMCA for a pickup game of basketball. They played a couple of games before taking a break to catch up with each other. They all took a seat on the benches in the gym as they watched other grown men and teenagers running up and down the court sweating profusely. They turned to face one another in a semicircle so that they could hear through the bouncing balls and the constant yelling. They began engaging in a typical schoolboy conversation.

"What's been going on, good brother?" Jason asked Vince.

"Man, you know me, work, work, and more work. I just got a promotion though," Vince responded.

"Hard work pays off, my dude. Congratulations," Randall chimed in.

"What are you going to be doing now, owning the place?" Demetrius asked.

"I'm going to be on the senior management team as Vice President for the department that handles corporate mergers and acquisitions. I 'll have a whole staff reporting to me and a lot more traveling responsibilities," Vince said.

"You making major moves now. How does the wife feel about all of that traveling though?" Randal asked.

Vince looked at Jason, took a sip of Gatorade before he responded to Randal and said, "Bro, I'm getting a divorce."

"Damn, I thought you found the one. You had us out here looking for Mrs. Right after that speech you gave about her at your engagement party and shit," Demetrius said.

"It's wild because the way you used to be with women back in the day I couldn't believe that you even settled down to begin with. I was happy you finally found that one who made you want to change," Jason interjected.

"Yeah, he was Mr. ladies' man. You did a total one eighty from who you used to be out here in these streets when you started dealing with her. Shit, if I had your old rotation I would have never settled down," Randal commented while slapping five with the others.

"Man, I think I changed a little too much for her to be honest. I don't want to get into what happened with me and Kyla but just know that your boy is back," Vince said as he stood up to join in the aggressive slapping of fives with the other fellas, then he continued, "I met this bad chick a couple of weeks ago and, let's just say, I showed her what the ladies couldn't get enough of back in the day. I'm about to stack my bench again."

"Yeah, that's how you move on bro, seriously. Get you a couple of bad chicks to add to your bench and keep it moving. I'm trying to change myself but every time *I* try to move on from my ex. though, I can't seem to meet a woman without kids. It's like, I have "rent-a-pop" written on my forehead," Demetrius said.

"You must be giving off that daddy vibe," Jason responded.

"I'm not trying to but you know I love the kids. But for real though, I just want to kick it without any restrictions but when they have kids, that's a no go. Shit's stressful man. I gotta help them with babysitting arrangements and shit," Demetrius said while laughing.

"I can't complain about meeting women with kids because I have one of my own so who am I to judge her? Hell, *I* might be the one looking for babysitting arrangements one day," Vince said.

"Change is good though; it's essential for growth and we ain't getting no younger," Jason said.

"Change for the right reason *or* the right woman is the key though Jay," Vince said.

"Just because it didn't work with Kyla, doesn't mean that the change wasn't worth it to make you a better man," Jason said.

"You always gotta be philosophical and shit, but you be on point," Randall said.

"Seriously bro, all bullshit aside, are you really over Kyla man?" Jason asked.

"Honestly, I don't think I'll ever be fully over her for a minute. I love that girl but I gotta do what I gotta do," Vince responded.

"Yeah, I hear you but from one married man to another, I just want you to think clearly about what you're doing because we all get hurt and we all go through things and I know as men our pride and ego can get the best of us and will even drive us to make mistakes that we might not be able to come back from is all I'm saying," Jason said.

"Damn, that was deep," Randall said.

"Yeah, had me thinking about my relationship and shit," Demetrius responded.

"I'm just keeping it real," Jason ended.

"Dr. Phil, can you help me with my relationship issues next?" Demetrious joked and they all laughed.

The fellas got back onto the court and continued their game a little while longer. Once it was over they all hugged it out and parted ways to head home. Vince couldn't get Jason's last words off of his mind as he walked to his car. Doubt began to creep back in again. Every time someone asked him if he still loved her, he always responded, "yes", but why couldn't he bring himself to forgive her? If forgiveness was even going to be possible, he had to face whatever it was that was holding him back from it but he wasn't sure what it was or if he would ever be ready. While he was in mid-thought, he felt a tap on his shoulder and turned around to see that it was the young lady from the elevator last week. He tried to be inconspicuous as he looked down at her breasts being supported in that sports bra and those colorful tights hugging her small waist and ample bottom. This was a welcomed distraction from where his head was.

"Did you forget about me?" she asked.

Not able to remember her name, he smiled and responded, "Not at all, beautiful."

"I haven't heard from you since I gave you my number."

Having no real excuse, he replied, "My apologies, I've been traveling for work."

"Okay, now that you're back, I'm ready for my dinner."

"I'm ready to take you up on that offer. What are you doing later?"

"I have plans tonight. How about you call me later and we can schedule a date?"

89

"Text me when you are free to talk."

"Okay, I will," she said as she smiled from ear to ear, then slowly turned to walk away.

As he watched her walk away he shook his head in admiration of her assets. It was really too bad that he couldn't remember her name but with so much going on and so many people coming at him at once, he just didn't take the time to commit her name to memory. He continued on to his car and headed home. Once he got inside he threw his keys on the table and they landed on the letter that Kyla hand delivered. Just as he was about to reach down for it, his phone rang.

"Hey mom," Vince said.

"Vincent, when are you going to bring my grandbaby over here to see me?"

"Well, hello to you too. She's with her mother this weekend, mom."

"This thing with you and Kyla needs to get worked out because I don't feel like I need to negotiate time with my grandbaby."

"I understand mom. Why don't you call her so she can bring her over there to see you?"

"I don't want to get involved in this mess between you two."

"I'm not asking you to get involved, I'm telling you that if you want to see Melanie you just need to call Kyla and she'll bring her over."

"That girl hasn't shown her face around here ever since you told her that you wanted a divorce so what makes you think that she is just going to up and bring the baby over here to me. She's probably embarrassed."

"Mom, you know how Kyla is; she is a fighter. She probably stayed away because she doesn't want to have to deal with you and end up making things worse."

"I *thought* I knew how she was but apparently I don't. I guess she knows that I have some words for her but that doesn't mean that I don't still love her as the mother of my grandbaby."

"Okay mom, I will call her and tell her that you want to see Melanie and to call you. Will that work for you?"

"Okay, sweetheart."

"Alright, mom. Love you."

"Love you too, son."

Vince hung up the phone with his mom and hopped in the shower. After he got out, he laid across the bed and fell immediately asleep for a midday nap.

* * *

It was a beautiful Saturday afternoon; the temperature was just right for a summer day with a cool breeze coming through the opened window of the family room. Kyla has just finished cleaning and organizing things around the house so she decided to take Melanie outside for a bit to play in the yard. As she sat there watching her daughter play with such happiness, the phone rang. She was hesitant to answer when she saw the Caller ID. Finally, after three rings, she picked up.

"How can I help you?" Kyla asked sarcastically.

"You don't really want to know the answer to that question," Sal responded.

"Whatever. What's up?"

"I was calling to see how things were going with your little get back together mission."

"Funny. You know you don't really give a damn about that or him."

"You're right, but I do give a damn about you, so I just wanted to make sure things were cool on *your* end since the way we left things or shall I say, the way *you* left things was a bit abrupt. You *literally* left a brother hanging."

"I'm sorry again, I still can't believe the way I let things get out of hand because I was confusing my feelings again. But I was clear on what I wanted to do at the time. Unfortunately, he and I just aren't on the same page with that at this point."

Sal started smiling and felt no remorse for not feeling bad that things weren't working out between Kyla and Vince.

"It's too bad that you didn't know that he wasn't going to be on the same page the night you were at my house. At least you could've gone home a much happier woman than you sound now," Sal added.

"Really? That's what you say to someone who is *clearly* in need of encouragement."

"I can give you some encouragement."

"I don't need your kind of encouragement."

"Sure you do; everyone needs my kind of encouragement."

"That's your problem now: it's not exclusive. I don't want what everybody can have."

"It can be all yours for a fee."

"A fee?"

"Nah, I'm just messing with you. Seriously though, what are you doing this afternoon?"

"Nothing, why?"

"I'm taking my son to Chuck E. Cheese's on the Boulevard; you and Melanie should join us."

"Damn, that's clear across town from us. What time?"

"You can meet me there at 4:00 to give you some time to get ready and get there. You should wear those jeans you had on that day I saw you too," Sal said laughing.

"I don't think so, buddy, this is a family friendly trip."

"You can't blame a brother for trying though."

"I can always expect you to try."

"You know me."

"Okay, I'll see you later."

Kyla and Sal hung up and she took Melanie in the house and they both changed clothes to meet Sal and Aaron. Summer traffic on Saturdays was always a nightmare on the Expressway so it took her longer than expected to get to Chuck E. Cheese's. When she pulled into the parking lot, she saw Sal and Aaron waiting outside by the entrance. She took a deep breath and got out of the car. Sal smiled and Kyla thought he looked damn near irresistible. He had on a plain white t-shirt that hugged his muscles perfectly with a pair of stonewashed jeans that sat neatly on his waist, a red Phillies cap that was turned slightly, covering his curly locks, and a pair of red and white Air Jordans. Kyla looked over to observe little Aaron wearing the same outfit. Although Kyla thought it was cute, she wondered if she and Melanie missed the twin memo over the phone because nothing about their outfits were matching. As they approached the entrance, Sal reached out and gave Kyla a hug and a kiss on the cheek. Aaron stared at her awkwardly without saying a word but Melanie waddled over to him as if she knew him and he started to smile.

"Are you ready to go in?" Sal asked.

"Sure, lead the way," Kyla awkwardly responded. This was the first time that she was going on a family outing with Sal and their children.

"I'll go get all of the tokens, you can go find us a table."

"Okay," Kyla said as she picked Melanie up to go searching for an empty table through the sea of people. Just as she was about to give up on her search for an empty table there was a family of four getting up and offered her their space. Sal and Aaron were making their way over to where Kyla and Melanie were waiting to sit down.

As Sal approached the table with Aaron and the family finally made their move, the gentleman turned to Sal and said, "That's a beautiful family you have there."

Sal not knowing what else to say, responded, "Thanks, man."

"How do you want to play this? It's so much going on in here so I feel like we need to take turns going to play or we might lose this table."

"That's cool. I will let Aaron go over there and play this row of games next to us where I can see him while you and Melanie go and do something."

"Well it's not much she *can* do here so we will go over and play in the ball pit for a while."

"Do want me to order the pizza while you're gone?"

"Sure."

"Cool."

Kyla picked Melanie up and went over to the ball pit and they both got in. Melanie was throwing colorful plastic balls around and clapping with excitement. Kyla's heart was getting so warm watching her daughter act this excited. These are things she didn't do with her normally because she'd been too busy drinking, wallowing in self-pity, and chasing Vince around. Now she saw how important this time with Melanie was because she could never get these memories back.

Sal watched Kyla and Melanie playing and saw the joy on both of their faces and began to think about the child they would've had together and if she would have been this kind of mother as a teenager. He was hoping to keep her smiling for as long as he could but he knew it was only temporary. Aaron ran over to him and asked if he could go over to the ball pit with the lady, referring to Kyla, and Sal agreed. He watched him run over to Kyla and as she picked him up to put him in there with them, his heart nearly melted even more because he had been raising him as a single dad and could see that Kyla was a great mom. At that very moment, the guy's last words before he gave up the table hit him and he thought about how this could be his family if he played his cards right in the long run. He

93

was careful not to bring women around Aaron because he didn't want him to get attached to someone who wouldn't be around for the long haul, but Kyla was different. He considered her to be family, even if they weren't ever going to be together.

She played with both of the kids for a while longer and then they all came back to the table when she saw the pizza being delivered. They all took a minute to wait for it to cool down before digging in. Sal and Kyla randomly locked eyes and felt as if they were staring into each other's souls. She was starting to feel something for him again, although she tried to fight it because she really couldn't afford to get sucked back in at this point. While trying to resist catching any feelings, she began to wonder if he would be different as a family man or if he could really be husband material. She started to question why she didn't choose to spend the rest of her life with him since it appeared that she was only going to end up here in the end anyway, which was starting to look like the case since Vince wasn't backing down from the divorce.

After they were done eating, Sal got up to go play more games with Aaron on the other side of the building. Kyla cleaned up the table and figured they no longer needed to hold on to it since they had already eaten so she put Melanie's baby bag on her shoulder and proceeded to the big sliding board. She thought that taking a few slides down with Melanie would be fun. As she stood in the line, she could see Sal and Aaron playing games and looking very much into it. Once she and Melanie reached the top of the sliding board, Kyla looked over again but didn't see Sal, only Aaron. After they made the trip down the colorful winding slide, with Melanie yelling from excitement, Kyla collected her things and headed over to where she saw Aaron.

As she approached, she saw Sal closely talking to a woman. Kyla slowed down her pace to see if Sal would even notice her coming but he didn't. In the blink of an eye, she and Melanie were standing next to him. The young woman looked Kyla up and down in a confrontational manner. Kyla looked back as if to say, "Is there a problem," with her eyes.

The young woman simply leaned in towards Sal's ear and said, "Call me tonight, okay."

With a sly grin on his face he said, "Okay, I will."

In that moment, Kyla felt like he hadn't changed a bit and this whole day was a fantasy that ended abruptly like a scratched record at a party so she got in his face and said, "Melanie's getting cranky so I think we better go."

"Or are *you* getting cranky?" Sal countered.

"Why would I be getting cranky?" She responded with an attitude.

"Look, Kyla, you can keep it real with me. I know you're salty about me talking to that chick but you don't even know what we were talking about or who she was to me to be jumping to conclusions and stomping off in your feelings like you always do."

"I'm not in my feelings," she said with an eye roll.

"That doesn't even matter honestly because I'm a single man, free to talk to or date whoever I want. If I can recall correctly, about two weeks ago, you ran out of my place practically naked telling me that you want to make it work with your husband. When he didn't want that shit, you started getting stars in your eyes today. Make up your fucking mind."

"So, you're telling me that you didn't feel something today."

"I never said that I didn't but we were chilling, just going with the flow. As usual, you go from zero to sixty. What I felt today shouldn't even be a discussion because you don't even take my feelings seriously anyway. If you did, you wouldn't have gotten married in the first place."

"That's not fair."

"The truth hurts don't it?"

"Since we're dropping truth bombs, you never took *me* seriously; so why did you *really* ask me to come here today?"

"Because I wanted to spend time with you and your daughter. What's so wrong with that?"

"Nothing, but if you're going to be getting numbers from other women in my face, that's not cool."

"We didn't come here as a couple; we came here as friends and again, you are jumping to conclusions about what happened with the woman."

"I hear you, but from where I was standing that's what it looked like."

"It doesn't matter what it looked like because that's not what it was but if you want to run away as you always do, that's up to you. I'm not gonna argue with you and I can't hold you or your feelings hostage. I'm waving the white flag so when you're ready to face things like a grown-up, then come and holler at me," he finished talking and grabbed Aaron's hand to head toward the door.

95

She watched him walk away, thinking that he would actually stop and wait for her, but he didn't and instead headed out the door. Kyla tried to catch up with him. When she finally made it through the crowd of people with Melanie in her arms, she exited looking around for Sal but he seemed to be gone. As she walked toward her car, a black Mercedes-Benz with tinted windows pulled up next to her and rolled down the window, startling her.

"I just wanted to make sure that you got in your car safely," Sal said.

"Thanks," Kyla said, without even turning to look at him.

"See, I'm not a complete asshole."

"Whatever."

Laughing, Sal responded, "There you go with your whatevers again."

"Why do you always have to point them out?"

"Because it's still cute and that's how I know the cat got your tongue, like I told you before."

"I can't deal with you right now."

"Maybe not right now but you will eventually so I'm not worried."

"You play too many mind games for me."

"No, I just know *you* and you know that I'm right. I'm in here, Ann," he said laughing, as he reached up to touch the side of her temple with his index finger.

"I don't know anything right now except that I'm taking my baby home. Have a good night, Salvatore," Kyla said as she strapped Melanie into her car seat and then hopped in the driver's side.

"Good night, Kyla Marie Carter," Sal said as he watched her drive off and then immediately followed.

"It's STILL Preston asshole," she yelled out the window as she drove away.

"I can't tell," he yelled back as he sped past her car.

The sun was beginning to set as early evening was approaching. Kyla was barely out of the parking lot onto the road to get home when the phone rang on her Bluetooth speaker system in her car. She figured it was Sal so she answered quickly and yelled, "What now?"

"What now?" Vince said confused.

"Wait, who is this?" Kyla said trying to clean things up a bit when she heard him speak.

"Don't you have caller ID?"

"It wasn't working for some reason and someone was playing on my phone. What's up?"

"My mom wants you to bring Melanie over?"

"When?"

"I don't know, you can call her and work all of that out."

"Can't you take her over there on one of your weekends?"

"You can't keep running from my family forever."

"Nobody's running from your family and why is that today's buzz word?"

"What are you talking about?"

"Never mind. I love your parents but of course they are all Team Vincent right now, hell my *own* parents are Team Vincent, so I'm staying out of the way of everybody."

"We are going to have to be around each other's families for the next eighteen years and beyond as co-parents so we need to get this out of the way, especially with Melanie's first birthday coming up."

"I'm just not ready to deal with your mom right now. Your dad doesn't say too much but your mom is a lot to handle and I don't want to start anything. I'll go if you come with me."

"No, because that will only confuse things and complicate the situation."

"Okay, but we still need to meet to discuss Melanie's birthday party anyway."

"We can talk about it tomorrow when you drop Melanie off for the week."

"Okay cool."

"Talk to you later," Vince said and hung up.

Kyla continued driving home, thinking that this was the first civilized conversation that she had with Vince since the divorce petition was served months before. Dr. Ellis told her that if she stopped forcing herself on him then maybe he would come around. She thought that perhaps this was a sign that he was ready to hear her out or that he'd read her letter. Suddenly, her eyes lit up. She was keeping hope alive because he was willing to sit down and have a face to face conversation with her tomorrow. She thought about how she could steer the conversation from the party into one about them. But something Sal said came to mind about how she always goes from zero to sixty with every situation and just can't go with the flow. She shook her head at the thought of how well he really *does* know her. She knew, though, they were so much alike and that it always seemed dysfunctional and exhausting how they carried on when they were together. Kyla got home, bathed Melanie, poured a glass of wine and spent the rest of her evening with the Lifetime Movie Network.

* * *

After Vince hung up the phone, he went to pull out some clothes from his closet to drop off at the cleaners on Monday and Liz's debit card fell out of one of his pant pockets onto the floor. He picked it up and looked at it for a second before texting her to let her know that he had it and could drop it off to her. She told him that she would be home later this evening and he could swing by then. He went on gathering his clothes and putting them in a bag before going to the kitchen to check the refrigerator for leftovers. Realizing that he was truly living like a bachelor and that he no longer had a wife to cook for him like he was used to, he threw on a pair of grey sweatpants, grabbed his house keys and headed out the door to walk to the grocery store. While walking, he looked up to the beautiful dusk sky and thought about his life. He wondered how he could allow himself to love this hard and get so caught up with a woman. She was consuming him at the most inopportune times and he wanted that to stop but couldn't figure out how to make it go away. Annette deserved his undivided attention the night that he was there but instead he thought about Kyla. He convinced himself that he had to get back to who he was before he met her. He realized, however, that if Jason was right, he might be a changed man and there would be no going back. Maybe Kyla made him a better man in the long run, but for some other woman. He still desired to have a family and even thought about giving marriage another shot in the future when he was mentally ready and completely moved on from Kyla.

He arrived at the store and picked up groceries and baby friendly foods for Melanie's week-long visit. On his way back to the apartment, he stopped for some Thai food at a place just across the street from him. He made it back upstairs to put the groceries away, turned on the Phillies game and started eating when Liz called his phone and told him that she was back. He told her that he would be down there in about a half an hour. After watching a few innings of the game, he grabbed his keys along with her debit card and headed out the door. Despite living on the same street, a few blocks apart, he never ran into Liz outside of the law firm for some reason, which was a good thing. He arrived at her building and buzzed her door and she let him up. When she opened the door she had on a short revealing night shirt and he knew that trouble was brewing.

"Come on in," Liz said, but he was reluctant to come inside because he could see that she had something up her missing sleeves.

"I just came to drop off your debit card and get back to watching the game," Vince said.

"Come on, I won't bite. I was actually just watching the game myself."

He came inside and saw that her TV was turned to the game as well and asked, "What's the score?"

"Phillies up 3-1 at the top of the 5th, bases are loaded with Howard up to bat."

"Ahhh, you know your baseball."

"Yeah, I used to play softball in high school and college."

"That's what's up. I used to play baseball from little league to high school. I would've played in college but I got hurt my senior year in high school and gave it up to crunch numbers."

"Damn, that's too bad, you might've been a star by now."

"Who knows?"

"You want something to drink?"

"What you got?"

"How is Tequila?"

"You went straight for the hard stuff. You not gonna ease me in with juice or nothing huh?" Vince said laughing.

"Why waste time on juice when you can have tequila shots," Liz said with a seductive smile.

"Shit, it's not like I'm driving," he said as he walked over to the kitchen island and took a seat at the bar stool.

As Liz poured the drinks she said, "Thank you for bringing my debit card over, it's one I don't normally use so I didn't even know it was missing until yesterday. I was looking all over for it today as a matter of fact and was about to cancel it just before you called me."

Not believing any of that, Vince responded as he took a sip of tequila, "Wow, what a coincidence."

"How is the world of accounting coming?"

"I'm not an accountant, I'm an analyst. But work is cool."

"Well, you work with numbers so it's all the same to me basically."

"I do more than working with numbers," he said getting a little annoyed at how dismissive she was about his career.

"Why are you in the house on a Saturday night?"

"I didn't have any plans tonight and Melanie is with her mom. Why are you home?"

"Because you're here," she said as she peeked at him through her glass.

Vince began to feel completely uncomfortable with where this evening was going. Liz kept walking around the kitchen, reaching for things that were up high and revealing her red thong underwear. He could see her erect nipples poking out of the shirt and he knew that it was time to go. They continued to have more small talk and a few more shots of tequila before he headed out.

He attempted to get up from the bar stool and said, "I need to get back to my place, I have to be somewhere early in the morning. Thanks for the drinks."

Liz didn't respond and blocked him from getting up as she came around to the front of the bar stool to straddle him. Once she sat facing him in his lap she attempted to kiss him but he pulled away.

"Yo, what are you doing?"

"What does it look like?" she responded as she tried again to kiss him but he again refused.

"It looks like you trippin' right now and perhaps had one too many shots of tequila. You *do* know that you're Kyla's best friend right."

"Ex-best friend. Besides, she doesn't deserve you."

"And you do?"

"Why not? I've heard all about this thing and I like what I've heard," she responded as she began to repeatedly rub her hands down the front of his sweatpants on to his manhood and she could tell that he was getting aroused because sweatpants don't lie and neither does tequila.

He reached his hands around her waist and picked her up and placed her feet flat onto the floor. Still determined to get him to want her, she pulled the night shirt over her head and dropped it at his feet. His eyes briefly lit up when he saw her standing there basically naked but he quickly looked away and said, "Put your clothes back on." She bent down to reach for the shirt but instead grabbed the front of his sweatpants and before he knew it she had her warm wet mouth placed firmly around his manhood and then pleasuring him with her tongue. As much as he wanted her to stop he felt paralyzed. She began going up and down like she was bobbing for apples so he just threw his head back in amazement and put his hands behind him to grab onto the bar stool to have something to hold on to. The deeper she went he started thinking that this must be her specialty because she had some serious skills and his knees were getting weak. The closer he came to climaxing, the more he tried to get her to stop. But she wouldn't, so he let go and she caught it in her mouth. After she was finished she looked up at him to see if he was ready for the real thing but he didn't make eye contact with her. She felt disappointed but figured that since he had gotten a taste of what she had to offer, he would be back. He pulled his pants back up, quietly grabbed his keys and headed for the door.

"Aren't you going to say goodbye?"

He looked down and just shook his head, opened the door and said, "This never happened."

"Oh, it happened. I just sucked your dick and judging from the happy ending, you liked it. I'm pretty sure you've *never* had your dick sucked like that before," she responded salaciously.

"If that's what you think," he said as he walked out and closed the door behind him.

Vince headed home. The two block walk felt like three miles. How was he ever going to explain this to Kyla because she was still his wife for the time being and Liz was supposed to be her best friend? There was no way she wasn't going to say anything but, he hoped that she would keep it secret. All types of scenarios started running through his mind from blackmail to hush sex. He should've seen this coming but when you have a half of a bottle's worth of tequila shots, anything is possible. He knew that she was wild but he didn't' think she was wild enough to do what she just did. He felt like he just left a prostitute and it didn't make him feel good. He made it home, took another shower to temporarily wash away the guilt and went to bed.

Chapter 9

It was Sunday morning and the sound of thunder startled Kyla and stole her from a restless sleep. She had tossed and turned all night anticipating her visit with Vince. She was acting as if it were their first date; in fact, she wished she could go back to that moment in time. The rain began coming down hard as she got out of the bed to go get Melanie for breakfast. When she went into Melanie's room, she noticed that she was still asleep, which was unusual for her because she stuck to a pretty consistent schedule. She figured that all of the playing at Chuck E. Cheese's must have worn her out so she shut the door and went downstairs to make breakfast. While in the kitchen she looked out the window and watched the rain come down when suddenly she was reminded again of the day that Vince walked out on her in the rain. She took a deep breath and got breakfast started but as soon as the eggs hit the pan she heard Melanie's cries signifying that she was awake.

Kyla hurried the eggs and put them to the side and ran up to get Melanie. Once she picked her up from the crib and placed her on the changing table to give her a clean diaper she began playfully talking to her and making clapping gestures while saying things like, "We're going to see daddy today. Are you excited? Mommy's excited too." Melanie was overcome with laughter for some reason and totally oblivious to her family's dynamic right now. Kyla scooped Melanie up and took her down to the kitchen to feed her breakfast.

Once they were fed, they went upstairs to get dressed. Kyla put on a beautiful long maxi dress that accentuated her curves. She packed Melanie's things for the week, called Vince to let him know that they were on their way, and then the two headed into the city. While driving, Kyla was listening to music when, suddenly, India Arie's "Ready for Love" came on and she began to sing the song with such passion that Melanie began to babble along. That song touched her soul and captured how she was feeling as she drove to Vince's house. She hoped that he was ready because she was ready for them to love again. As she got closer, she started to get butterflies in her stomach because she wanted this conversation to go well since so many others before this one didn't. She pulled onto his street and searched for parking. She found a spot about a half a block from his apartment. She parked, grabbed Melanie and the bags, and headed to Vince's apartment. Once he opened the door, Melanie stretched her arms out for him and he took her from Kyla.

"How's daddy's baby?" Vince asked Melanie.

Melanie smiled and clapped as he kissed her on the forehead before putting her down in the gated play area so he could talk to Kyla.

"Aren't you going to ask how Melanie's mommy is?" Kyla said laughing as she took a seat on the couch.

"I was getting to that," Vince said, as he sat beside her and threw his cellphone on the table.

"Sure you were."

"So what's going on?"

"Nothing much really. You?" Kyla said, taking the conversation slowly.

"Not too much myself. I've been working like crazy lately. I just got a promotion."

"Oh wow, congratulations. What will you be doing now?"

"Dealing with mergers and acquisitions. They asked me to run the department as the new VP."

"That's major. I'm really proud of you; you're a hardworking man and deserve a shot up the corporate ladder," she said with a huge smile not knowing whether or not a hug would be appropriate.

"Thanks, I really appreciate it. So what's the plan for Melanie's birthday?"

"I was thinking that we could have a party in the park. We could rent a pavilion and have moon bounces, face painting and pony rides."

"All that for a first birthday? She won't even remember it," he said, as he got up to walk into the bathroom.

"Yeah, you only get one first birthday so we have to do it right," she yelled so that he could hear her in the nearby bathroom.

Just as she was waiting for him to respond, a text message appeared across his phone and the name above it made her do a double take. She intended to ignore the text but she decided to pick the phone up to see what the message said. Once she read it, her face turned red and her blood began to boil.

Vince emerged from the bathroom and said, "I was thinking we could..."

She cut him off in mid-sentence, held his phone out towards him and calmly said, "Explain this."

"Explain what?"

"This text message from Liz," she yelled.

He immediately got a lump in his throat and calmly asked, "Why are you going through my phone?"

"I wasn't going through your phone, it was sitting here and I could see the message on the screen and I didn't like what I read."

"What did you read?"

"There's more where last night came from with a tongue emoji. What the fuck is that supposed to mean?"

"I don't know."

"Since you're so clueless, then what happened *last night* that you need more of huh?"

"Nothing happened. I dropped off her debit card."

"Why the hell did you have her debit card?"

"She left it at the restaurant when we had lunch."

"LUNCH! So what you seeing this bitch now?"

"No, I'm not seeing her. It wasn't that serious, she saw me downtown and asked me to lunch."

"And she *conveniently* left her debit card so you could find it and bring it to her house?"

"I'm telling you that's all that happened."

"Do I look like a fucking fool? The text message *clearly* says something else happened last night and I know Liz."

"We had drinks."

"And…"

"Talked."

"But I thought you just dropped off her debit card. Did you sleep with her because I swear to GOD if you did…"

"You're gonna do what?" Vince said boldly.

"I'm gonna bury both of y'all," Kyla said loudly as she pointed a finger in his face.

"Hold the hell up, you trippin right now and you're not burying *anyone* so you can get the hell outta here with *that* bullshit after you were out here fucking some other dude."

"This ain't about Sal right now, this is about *you* fucking my best friend to get back at me."

"Why would I do that? If I wanted to get back at you, I would just divorce you, like I'm already doing."

"I don't believe that one bit and I'm about to go over there and ask her ass."

"You can do whatever you want but I'm telling you, I didn't have sex with that girl."

"Well, what *did* you do with her?

"Look I already told you what we did and I don't owe you any explanations either. You can't come up in here reading my messages and threatening me. We're not together because of something *you* did but yet you think you have some type of authority to regulate what *I* do."

"I am *still* your wife, whether you choose to believe that or not. I came over here to have a civilized conversation about our daughter's birthday and see what else we might be able to hash out but I see you have other plans. I'm telling you now that if I find out that you and Liz are sleeping together, I will destroy both of you!"

"Are you threatening me?"

"No, I'm promising you," Kyla said as she got up and snatched her purse off of the couch.

Kyla walked over to Melanie in the playpen, leaned over to give her a kiss and said, "Be good for daddy. I love you," before walking out of the apartment and slamming the door behind her. Vince just stood there with his heart beating because he didn't expect Kyla to find out this way or this fast and he genuinely felt bad about it but he wasn't going to stand for her threatening him either. He knew that she wouldn't stop until she got to the bottom of what really happened so it was only a matter of time before she came back for more. He immediately picked up the phone and called Liz. She answered on the first ring.

"I knew you couldn't resist my offer," she said without a hello.

"Look, don't text or call my phone anymore," Vince said angrily.

"Damn, what's got your boxers in a bunch?"

"Kyla just left here and she saw your message."

"So."

"*So?* She is pissed and thinks I slept with you."

"You know you wanted to."

"No, I didn't. I let you do what you did because let's face it, I'm a man but I can't be responsible for her actions if she finds out, so you need to keep your mouth shut."

"I'm not afraid of Kyla but it sounds like *you* are."

"I'm not afraid of anybody and especially not her but she is still my wife and I don't need this drama right now in the middle of a divorce."

"Drama? You came to *my* place and from what I can tell you were down with it."

"Come on, don't act like a lot of drinks weren't involved and that you didn't manipulate the situation.

"So you're gonna blame it on the alcohol now? If she asks, I'm going to tell her the truth…wait, somebody's at my door," Liz said as she got quiet to look out of the peep hole. "This is her now, speaking of the devil," Liz continued with a devious laughter.

"I'm telling you, keep your mouth shut."

"Bye, Vince," Liz said as she hung up and began unlocking the door to let Kyla in.

Liz opened the door with an eye roll and said, "So to what do I owe this pop-up visit? Let me guess, you were in the neighborhood?"

106

"I think you know why I'm here," Kyla responded with an attitude.

"I'm afraid I don't."

"Let's cut the bullshit, Liz. Are you fucking my husband?"

"Wow, that's a leap. You're still calling him your husband?"

"That's because he *is* my husband."

"Funny, that's not what he told me."

"I don't care *what* he told you. He'll tell you anything to get what he wants."

"Well, from what I can tell, he doesn't want *you* based on last night."

"Oh and you think he wants *you*? You're a washed up whore who will sleep with anybody."

"And you're a cheating liar who doesn't deserve to be with a man like Vince."

"You know what, bitch, I'm not even going to dignify that with a response."

"You don't have to respond, because you know it's true."

"What I do know is that you are a pathetic excuse for a woman and I should have listened to my sister and cut you off a long time ago. She said you were jealous of me and wanted my life and you couldn't wait to get it. Well I hope that you got what you wanted because he's never going to be with you. You are a cheap slut with no morals who will never be happy."

"I'm not the one that's unhappy; I believe that is you. You're the one standing in *my* living room questioning me about sleeping with *your* soon-to-be ex-husband. Last night I gave your *so-called* husband a happy ending that I believe he'll never forget. And as for me being a pathetic excuse for a woman, I'm not the one that cheated on her husband repeatedly and got pregnant multiple times by another man."

"Get your facts straight. Vince wasn't my husband when any of that happened but last night when you were giving out your famous happy ending, he *was* my husband and you crossed the line."

"Well he crossed it right along with me."

"I'm going to deal with him but as for you, we're done. You're dead to me and if I didn't need my livelihood, you'd *really* be dead," Kyla said as she reached for the doorknob to let herself out.

"That's fine, because you've *been* dead to me so there is no love lost here," Liz responded matter-of-factly.

Just as Kyla was about to exit Liz's apartment she turned around and punched Liz in the face so hard that Liz fell backward onto the couch and blood started leaking from her nose. She stood there for a second contemplating jumping on her and continuing to beat her senselessly but she knew that, because she was so enraged, she had to walk away to keep from hurting her and going to jail so she walked out and slammed the door. Liz sat there in a state of confusion from the blow that she had just been dealt to the face but resolved herself the fact that she deserved it. Kyla went to her car and sped away in a fit of rage.

* * *

Alexis was busy in the kitchen cleaning chicken when she heard the doorbell ring repeatedly, followed by hard knocking. She wondered whether or not it was an emergency and she dropped the chicken into the sink as she rushed to the door. When she looked out of the peephole, she saw Kyla standing there with tears rolling down her face so she quickly snatched the door open.

As she was opening the door, she heard Chris yell downstairs, "Who is that?"

She yelled back, "It's Kyla, babe."

"Is everything okay?" Chris questioned.

"I'm about to find out," Alexis finished as Kyla stepped inside.

"Let me know if you need me."

"I will.

Alexis took one look at Kyla and saw that she was a mess so she just pulled her into an embrace and said, "Is everything okay, sis? Talk to me."

Kyla just cried on her shoulder and through the tears responded, "You were right."

"Right about what?" Alexis responded as he led Kyla into the kitchen.

"Liz," she mumbled, as she cried out before taking a seat at the table.

"What did she do?" Alexis questioned angrily.

"She slept with Vince."

"She did what?"

"I saw a message from her on his phone when I went over there to drop Melanie off and it seemed shady like they were messing around so I asked him about it."

"What did he say?"

"He said he didn't sleep with her."

"So why do you think they slept together?"

"I went over to her place to confront her and she admitted it."

"She told you she slept with your husband?" Alexis yelled.

"No, she said she gave him a happy ending."

"What the hell is that supposed to mean?"

"That's her code for giving head."

"That nasty bitch! I'm about to go put my shoes on because she needs to be punched in her nasty ass mouth."

"I already punched her in the face."

"Oh no, that wasn't enough and I'm really surprised at my brother-in-law for doing that so he needs to be punched in his mouth too."

"I'm not surprised. He's been so mad at me lately that I think he would do anything to hurt me."

"The nerve of her! You don't do shit like that. Ooooh, that bitch!"

"You said she would do something like this and I didn't believe you but I'm officially done with her."

"I'm sorry that things have gotten this bad for you."

"Me too. I can't believe I fucked my life up like this. My life is really falling apart right now," Kyla said as she started crying again.

Alexis pulled her into an embrace to comfort her and said, "It's not the end of the world. I think you and Vince can still work this out after you punch *him* in the face."

"He doesn't seem to want to work this out ever and I've started to get tired of hoping, wishing and praying. After what just went down, I'm seriously thinking about just signing those papers and starting over. I will have to accept the fact that I failed at marriage and move on."

"You're not a failure, and I told you before that you're a fighter and this fight is about going the distance. It's not like you to give up on anything. This is just a set-back on your road to reconciliation."

"I tried to stay in this fight as long as I could but what he did was too low of a blow so I'm out but on my way out I plan to hit him below the belt; right in the pockets since he just got a big promotion. He's going to pay for this shit literally. He must've forgot who he married."

"Damn, that's a costly payback for him."

"Maybe I should have just stayed with Sal and none of this would have ever happened. I wouldn't have ruined Vince's life or mine."

"Now you're talking crazy. I know you're upset but that would have been a whole different set of problems."

"How?"

"After all you went through with him, do you think he would be anywhere near the marrying type?"

"I don't know because we never gave it a shot. He seems to be a changed man, especially since he had his son."

"He has a son now?"

"Yeah, Aaron is three. His ex-wife lives in Vegas and left Aaron with him when she figured out they weren't going to be together."

"So, he was married?"

"Yeah, briefly, but that's a long story."

"Why didn't it work?"

"Because he said that he wanted to be with me but I was already engaged to Vince when he made that declaration."

"So he left his wife for you and you still got married anyway? That's deep and explains why you took so long to go through with the wedding and why he showed up."

"It's a little more complicated than that."

"Well maybe you *should* give him a chance if you are really going to let this be over between you and Vince."

"I don't know anymore. I need to be by myself, figure out what I really want and then jump back out there in the dating world. I have to worry about Melanie and how she is going to be affected by this divorce."

"Are you going to talk to him and tell him that you talked to Liz?"

"No, it's a waste of time, he'll know when he gets the signed papers and the petition from my lawyer."

Chris magically appeared in the kitchen and said, "Is everything alright?"

Kyla looked up at him sheepishly and responded, "I'm going to be okay."

"I don't have to hurt nobody, do I?" Chris asked seriously.

Alexis responded, "You might need to go over there and talk to your brother-in-law."

"Did he put his hands on you?" Chris asked Kyla sternly.

"No, he's just running around here putting his married dick in places that it doesn't belong," Alexis said angrily.

"Oh, well I'm not getting in that fight. You ladies carry on," Chris said as he threw his hands in the air and left the kitchen.

"Men, they all stick together I swear," Alexis said with an eye roll.

"I'm going to go home and do some soul searching and figure out my next move."

"Okay sis, call me if you need me because you know I will be ready to run over there and beat Liz's ass in two seconds flat."

"I know you will," Kyla said as she stood up to give her sister a goodbye hug. Alexis watched Kyla as she got in the car and then shut the door.

* * *

Kyla arrived home and furiously pulled into her garage. The more she reflected on what had transpired today, the angrier she grew. She wanted to hurt somebody. Once she got inside her house, she hurried upstairs to her bedroom, rifled through her nightstand and pulled out the divorce papers. She read them over and over again about ten times. Once she got to the last time, she grabbed a pen, signed them and cried like she was attending a final viewing at a funeral. She tried to pull herself together but the pain was too great so she cried herself to sleep. When she woke up it was early evening and the sun hadn't gone down and she had a headache. Before she got up to get some pain relief, she thought about some other relief that she could use so she reached over for her phone, scrolled through and dialed. After nearly four rings there was an answer.

"Hello," Sal said.

"I want to see you tonight," Kyla said.

He looked over at the girl sitting across from him at the dinner table and responded, "What time?"

"How about 9:00?"

He excused himself from the dinner table and said, "That's perfect, it'll give me time to get home from running these errands."

"Come to my house."

"I don't know where you live."

"I'll text you the address."

"Are you sure that's a good idea."

"Melanie is with her dad for the week and it's my idea so it's a good one."

"Okay, I'll be there at 9:00."

Sal hung up the phone and returned to the dinner table with his companion and told her that something urgent had come up so he would be taking her home right after dinner. He received the address from Kyla and he was all set.

Kyla jumped in the shower and pulled herself together emotionally. She went to the kitchen and poured herself several glasses of wine while she waited in the family room watching television. Right as the clock displayed 9:00PM, the doorbell rang, and it was Sal. As soon as she opened the door, Sal took one look at her in a black see through robe and knew what this call was all about. She didn't even speak to him and they barely got the door closed before he threw her up against the wall in the doorway, interlocking his fingers with hers as he started to kiss her. After a few minutes she pushed him off of her and reached down to drop her robe to the floor. As she stood there with nothing on, Sal was once again in awe of her beauty and femininity and jumped right back into action. She wasn't going to turn back, she wanted this, and in fact she felt that she needed this. She didn't care about anybody's feelings at this moment because this moment was all about her. She stood pressed against the wall while he kissed up and down her body, heating her up like a microwave oven. He kissed her in all of the places that would make the hair stand up on the back of her neck. He slowly picked her up, carried her into what he perceived to be the living room area and gently placed her down on the rug in front of the empty fireplace. The moonlit sky coming through the picturesque window was the perfect backdrop to what was about to happen. She felt like it was going to be magical as she watched him remove his clothes in anticipation. He didn't want to waste time on foreplay because he remembered what happened the last time she was naked in front of him. He went right in for the kill.

Just as he was about to insert himself inside of her she stopped him and asked, "Do you have a condom?"

He looked puzzled because they had never used one before, he replied, "Yes, why do you ask?"

"I don't want any slip-ups this time."

"We've been doing this for many years and have never had a slip-up since we were teenagers but if that's what you want," he said as he reached into his pants pocket to get the condom.

It was clear that he was unaware of the second slip-up in Vegas, she responded, "I just want to be sure."

The wind had been taken temporarily out of his sail so he reached for her hands and placed them on his erection. She moved her hands up and down slowly stimulating him more and more, when suddenly he handed her the condom.

"What do you want me to do with that?" she questioned.

"Put it on for me."

"Wow, I've never done this before."

"It's a first time for everything and I always love being your first. We've never dealt with condoms since we've been together so this will be a new experience for the both of us."

Kyla fumbled with the gold foil packet to open it and tried to channel her high school sex education class to properly place it. Once she got it on she pushed him backward onto the carpet and climbed on top of him. He inserted himself into her and she began to travel up and down slowly with him gripping her waist to control her movements. He began to forcefully thrust upward with every downward stroke making it harder for her to control herself. She was moaning wildly as he was saying things like, "You couldn't stop thinking about this, could you?"

In the midst of so much pleasure she yelled out, "Yes!" Her speed was beginning to increase and he could feel himself reaching a breaking point so he pushed her backward to switch positions in mid stride and take control. Just like that, she ended up with her legs around his neck with him on his knees, hands around her waist and stroking her quickly and deeply. They were sweating and moaning so loudly that if her house was close enough to a neighbor, they would be heard through the walls. This pleasure-filled moment was coming to an end for her as she reached her climax, which only excited him more so he kept going as if he was going to plow right through her. It seemed that the more noise she made, the faster and harder he got. Just when she thought it was over, he switched positions again and re-entered her from behind. He bent her over, wrapped his hands around her breasts and pounded away until he reached his climax. They both collapsed to the floor out of breath. Kyla thought to herself that she made the right call because as usual, he doesn't disappoint. The two lay there silent and looking up at the ceiling. This was one of the rare times that she didn't feel any feelings for him in that moment. Perhaps she was still numb emotionally from what had just happened with Vince or maybe she was no longer emotionally connected to him. Either way, everything about this moment still felt good.

Finally, Sal broke the silence and said, "Damn, you certainly are a great hostess."

"Well, you are a great house guest," Kyla responded.

"I barely even got past the front door. I don't know where your room is so this was the best I could do."

"I can give you the grand tour when we get up off of the floor. This is the actual living room, although we don't ever come in here."

"It's a nice living room," Sal said as he looked around.

Kyla stood to her feet and reached her hand down to pull Sal up and said, "Let me show you to the bathroom."

Sal picked up his clothes and followed her to the stairs as he looked at all of the family photos on the walls. The one that stuck out for him was the large wedding photo hanging in the foyer area. Seeing that photo was like getting punched in the stomach even though he saw her get married. But the fact that he was standing in the home that she used to share with her husband was sort of redemptive for him. He felt like she was his. As far as he was concerned, Vince didn't deserve to have her. Once they got upstairs, she showed him to the guest bathroom where the towels were located. He went inside and washed up while she went into the bathroom in her room. Once he was dressed, he went inside of her bedroom and waited for her to come out of the bathroom.

She jumped when she saw him standing there and said, "You scared me."

"How? You knew I was in the house."

"I know but I wasn't expecting you to be in my room."

Looking around the room, Vince says, "So this is where the magic happens?"

"What magic?"

"Yeah, just like I thought: no magic."

"Was that supposed to be funny?"

"Nope. I told you before that I know that man ain't hittin it right."

"Why do you always say that?"

"Because I know."

"Based on?"

"It's a man thing."

"I don't know what you're talking about. You act like you are the only one with the 'magic'."

"I am and I don't see some dude named Vincent having any."

"Well, *Vincent* is busy giving his magic to my best friend."

"Damn, that's fucked up. She *is* fine though," Sal said laughing.

"What!" Kyla exclaimed as she punched him in the chest.

"Nah, I'm messing with you. He seemed like a good dude, I don't see him doing something like that. He was too straight laced."

"He did and I'm done with both of them."

"So that's why you called me?"

"No, I just wanted to see you."

"Really?"

"Yeah, no bullshit."

"That's usually me trying to get into your pants but I see my little Kyla Marie is growing up and taking control. Look at you," Sal said jokingly pinching her cheeks.

"Whatever."

"It's okay. Own your womanhood and be okay with just wanting to get yours. I don't mind if you call me up to give it to you. I'll gladly deliver."

"I bet you don't mind delivering. I need to get ready for work tomorrow."

"Damn, you putting me out? You just gonna hit and run huh?"

"No, that's not what I'm saying, I'm just about to get my routine started for tomorrow is all but you're welcome to stay."

"It's cool baby girl, I have to go get my son from my mom's house anyway so I will call you tomorrow," Sal said as he leaned over to kiss her on the cheek.

"I'll walk you out," Kyla said as she escorted him to the back door.

"I'm parked in the front."

"Oh, damn, Vince always uses the back door."

"I see where you head is."

"No that's not it, I made an honest mistake. We just never used the front door."

"It's all good. I'll talk to you."

"Okay, drive safe," Kyla said as they kissed goodbye.

Kyla shut and locked the door then went upstairs to get ready for work. Even though she felt good physically, mentally she was still a mess. But life had to go on.

Chapter 10

O n Monday morning Kyla strolled into work with a new found desire to hit the reset button on her life. With her career sliding down a slippery slope and her marriage basically over, it was time to put some things into perspective and hop back into the game of life with two feet. She took on a few new clients to keep herself busy at work. She closed three new deals and assisted with getting a new contract negotiated for a local television personality. While it was a busy day at work, she knew that she needed to get the ball rolling on the divorce papers. Once she got to a place where she could have some alone time, she sat at her desk and flipped through her Rolodex of attorneys to find the card for Mark Leibowitz, supposedly the best divorce attorney in the city. She knew that if she were going to take Vince down, she had to go to the best because his attorney wasn't a slouch either. She picked up her office phone and called the office of the attorney.

"Leibowitz, Stein, and Rowe, how may I direct your call?"

"Yes, hi, I'm trying to reach Mark Leibowitz."

"Please hold, let me see if Mr. Leibowitz is available."

"Thank you."

Kyla sat through about a minute of hold music before the receptionist returned and said, "Mr. Leibowitz is with a client right now but do you want to leave a message?"

"I'm trying to make an appointment with him, when is your next available?

"His next available is actually tomorrow at 4:00PM due to a recent cancellation. Do you want that one?"

"Yes."

"Your name?"

"Kyla Preston."

"Can I have your contact number in case we need to reach you?"

"Sure, you can reach me at the office at 215-555-9090.

"Okay, Ms. Preston, we'll see you tomorrow."

"See you then."

Kyla hung up and called her assistant Frank into her office. He walked in and sat down in front of her.

"You look more upbeat than I've seen you in a while. What's going on?" Frank asked.

"I had a good night is all," Kyla responded.

"You *slept* good?" he said with a sly grin.

"You could call it that," Kyla said with a vivid memory that gave her a momentary shake.

"So you got a new boo, huh?"

"Not exactly."

"Did Vince come over last night?" Frank said as he sat up in the chair waiting for the answer with baited breath.

"No, I had a visit from an old friend."

"Well he must've been a good friend because you came to work smiling and I haven't seen that in a while."

"You know what, Frank," Kyla said laughing.

"I'm just calling it like I see it."

"I need you to clear my schedule after 3:30 tomorrow. I need to leave for a meeting. Move some things around if you need to."

"Okay, I can do that."

"Thanks, Frank."

"You know I have your back."

"I know. You're the best."

Frank left Kyla's office and she sat back in her chair thinking about that smile on her face and how it got there. She pondered whether or not she could see him putting that smile on her face for the long term and snapped out of the thought when her office phone rang.

"Kyla Preston."

"Hey, girl," Alexis said.

"What's up sis?"

"I have two extra tickets to see Jill Scott Thursday night and wanted to know if you wanted to double date."

"Who am I going to give the second ticket to?"

"I think you know who to call."

"You're funny. I don't even know if he's available."

"All you have to do is ask."

"I don't know if I'm ready to do all of that."

"It's only a date. You've been dealing with him this long and aren't comfortable going on a date? You *have* been on dates with him before haven't you?"

Just in that moment, Kyla realized that her life with him had been so exclusive that the idea of letting people into their world was scarier than she'd thought. The whole allure of being with Sal was that it was just the two of them with no one else; no friends, no family or anyone to disturb their chemistry. Kyla responded, "We have been on dates, but never double dates."

"Well, there's a first time for everything. Give the man a call."

"Okay, I'll see what he says. Let me get back to work."

"Okay, sis."

Kyla hung up and went back to work until it was time for her to leave the office. She rushed home and gathered up any documents that she thought would be necessary for her lawyer to start putting together her side of the case. Once she got everything in order, she ate and watched television for a bit before attempting to fall asleep. She almost forgot about her sister's request for her to bring a date for the concert. She really wished she had someone else that she could call because she didn't want to get all caught up again with Sal. At this point, he was her only option. At least he was arm candy and she knew they would have a good time, if nothing else. She grabbed her phone and called him but he didn't answer so she left a message and fell off to sleep.

The next morning, Kyla woke up, got dressed, and put her game face on. She went into work and asked Frank to get her a meeting with Mr. Lee, the managing partner. He made a call to his assistant and was able to get her a lunch meeting at noon. Kyla spent the bulk of her morning reading contracts and following up with phone calls to occupy her time. While in the middle of redlining one of her contracts, her office phone rang and it was Mr. Lee's assistant confirming their lunch meeting and the location. She wrapped up everything and headed down to the restaurant early so she could have a clear head on what she planned to discuss with him. She arrived, got a table and the server brought her sparkling water. About fifteen minutes later, Mr. Lee arrived and joined her. She stood up when he walked in and extended her hand for a handshake. The server came over to take their orders and they continued on to their meeting.

"Thank you for meeting me for lunch on such short notice, sir," Kyla said.

"When one of my star players wants to meet, I felt like it was only right to make the time," Mr. Lee responded with a smile.

"I appreciate that and what you think of me. I asked for this meeting because I felt like I needed to be upfront with you about what's been going on with me lately that has taken my head out of the game."

"Okay, I'm listening."

"I've been dealing with some personal issues and I shouldn't have let them cause me to lose the momentum that I was gaining on my quest for a partnership, but I did. For that, I apologize. I am fully focused and ready to work hard."

"Are those issues resolved now?"

"Almost, but I have them under control."

"That's good to know because for a minute we were worried about you and your commitment to this firm. You do great work, bring in large volume but we've noticed some decline in your billable hours as well as your famous attention to detail that we've come to appreciate."

"I know and that is why I wanted to reassure you that the fire is back and I'm ready to work."

"Well, Mrs. Preston, I am certainly glad to know that we have your undivided attention again."

"Absolutely," Kyla finished as she held up her glass for confirmation.

They wrapped up their meeting and as she was walking out of the door, Devin Jackson, her strikingly handsome client from Chess Entertainment gently grabbed her by the hand as she was passing his table. She turned around to see who was touching her and noticed him.

"Hello, beautiful," Devin said.

"Hello, Mr. Jackson," Kyla responded.

"Still not mixing business and pleasure I see."

"Not at all."

"I can see that but since we don't have any business together at the moment, I wanted to say hello and remind you how beautiful I still think you are."

"So noted."

"When are you going to let me take you out?"

"Why do you want to take me out, Mr. Jackson?"

"Because I still never thanked you for all that you did for our company in New York a while back."

"That's why you hire a good entertainment attorney. I did my job and the fact that we still have your business is thanks enough."

"Maybe, but I want to *personally* thank you."

"Call my assistant to see what my schedule looks like."

"You don't know your own schedule?"

"I've been busy lately so I need to be sure I'm clear."

"I would prefer to call *you* directly, if that's okay."

"I guess I can do that," Kyla said as she gave him her personal cellphone number.

"I will be in touch and I promise you won't be disappointed," He said with a seductive grin.

"Let's hope not," she responded with a devilish grin of her own as she started towards the door.

"Take care beautiful."

"I have a name," Kyla said as she exited to head back to the office to finish out her day.

* * *

While waiting in Mr. Leibowitz's office, Kyla flipped through a few legal magazines until she saw an article that caught her eye about the practice. Just as she was getting into the article, Mr. Leibowitz's assistant come to show her to his office. Once inside, he stood up to shake her hand and offer her a seat.

"Mrs. Preston, what brings such a fine young attorney here to *my* office?" he asked.

"Well, Mr. Leibowitz, this fine young attorney needs the best divorce lawyer in the Tristate area because my husband has filed for divorce. Initially, I refused to sign the papers because I thought we could work it out; I've since changed my mind and decided to seek legal counsel."

"How long have you two been married?"

"Two years. And they've been a trying two years."

"Why did he file for divorce?"

"He found out that I had an affair with another man before we were married. He questioned the paternity of our daughter and made me get a DNA test and everything."

"It certainly *has* been a busy two years for you guys," he said as he read through the petition for divorce.

"To top all of that off, I just found out that he slept with my best friend."

"Now, that's a game changer. According to his petition, he is filing on the basis of irreconcilable differences and you disagreed with that initially?"

"Yes, I thought that we could work things out because I needed him to understand that I didn't cheat on him while we were married and what he read in the letters that he found happened in the past before we were even married but he refused to listen to me."

"Is there any chance that you could still reconcile?"

"At this point, I'm pretty sure the marriage is over, we have done too much to each other to save it."

"I've seen marriages that looked like the couple would kill each other if they stayed together ultimately come out on the other side even stronger with help from professionals. Maybe this is just a storm. Usually we try to start with mediation before jumping to divorce, if it could be salvageable."

"With all due respect sir, this is beyond just a storm, it's a tsunami and people usually don't survive those."

"Since you put it that way, it sounds like you don't see a chance to save it so we can skip the mediation option. I see here that he has retained Spencer Davis as his attorney. I've opposed him many times in divorces and he is tough, but I'm tougher."

"That's why I'm here."

"I'm your guy. What are you asking for in response to this petition?"

"I want the house to raise our daughter in, full custody and child support. He just got a big promotion so I also want spousal support as well. I brought in all of the support documents that you need to make your case."

"You're going for the jugular I see and you know that's going to be tough to get all of this since you haven't been married that long and he is claiming infidelity on your part."

"Yes, but I'm ready for the fight and technically, he's the one that was actually unfaithful during the marriage."

"I'll get started on my response to the petition and get my boxing gloves ready."

"Great."

"I will be in touch when it's ready so you can look it over before we send it to his attorney."

"Okay, I look forward to working with you, Mr. Leibowitz."

"Likewise Mrs. Preston, Mr. Leibowitz finished as they got up to shake hands before Kyla exited his office to head home.

* * *

Thursday arrived and Kyla still had not heard from Sal, despite several attempts to contact him. She decided to attend the concert without him. She couldn't understand why he wasn't responding to her calls or text messages and she was beginning to get worried because it wasn't like him to ignore her or be unresponsive. She reached into her closet and pulled out a hot little black dress with the back cut out and a pair of strappy shoes to compliment the dress. She got glammed up and headed out to meet her sister and brother-in-law at the concert. She parked her car and headed towards to entrance to meet up with them and as she approached the door she heard someone call her name from the window of a limo that was parked out in front of the entrance. She turned to see that it was Devin Jackson again. This was twice in one week but then it clicked that he *was* the CEO of an entertainment company.

"Hello again, beautiful," he said through the partially rolled down window.

She turned toward the car and said, "Hello again Mr. Jackson."

"Stop being so formal with me and just call me Devin."

"Okay, hello, Devin and you can call me Kyla."

"Hello, Kyla. You're going to the concert I see."

"Good guess."

"Alone?"

"Now why would I attend a concert alone?"

"I don't know; women do stuff like that."

"I'm meeting my sister and brother-in-law."

"Third wheel? Where's *your* date?"

"I don't have one but I since I enjoy Jill Scott so much, I couldn't pass up the ticket."

"Why don't you be my date?"

"Just like that, huh? What am I supposed to tell my sister? Besides, she has my ticket."

"You can tell her that you're with me and you don't need a ticket because I'm one of the promoters so you'll be in a box with me. In fact, tell your sister and brother-in law to join us as well. After the show we'll go backstage to meet Jill."

"Aren't you fancy?"

"Not really, but I do fancy a beautiful woman and wouldn't want you to be out here looking this good without someone on your arm," he said as he opened the door to get out of the limo.

"Okay, let me call my sister and tell her."

124

Kyla took out her phone and called Alexis to let her know that they would be upgrading to VIP and sitting with Devin. Alexis was excited as she and Chris navigated the crowd to meet up with her sister at the front gate.

"Devin, this is my sister Alexis and my brother-in-law Chris," Kyla said as they reached out to shake hands with him.

"Pleased to meet you and glad you will be joining me in my box," Devin responded as he showed his credentials to security and they followed him through the door.

Once inside the Wells Fargo Center, they went up the escalator to the box level and entered Box 16.

Alexis leaned over once they got inside and whispered to Kyla, "Where did you get this guy from? He's gorgeous."

Kyla whispered back, "Oh, he's one of my clients."

"I know we don't mix business with pleasure but ba-by, he is worth the risk," Alexis said giving her a secret high five off to the side.

"He's been trying to take me out for over two years but of course I was engaged and then married. But as of today…well, you know my status and I haven't heard from Sal."

"We have to keep all options open, so I say have a good night."

"Ladies," Devin said clearing his throat, interrupting their chatter off to the side."

"I'm sorry, I was just telling my sister something," Kyla said.

"I can see that. Drinks anybody?"

"Rum and coke for me," Chris said.

"I got the good stuff man," Devin responded.

"That's what's up," Chris replied.

"I'll have a glass of white wine," Kyla said.

"Same for me, Alexis responded."

Devin poured drinks for everyone and shortly after, a few of Devin's employees joined them. The house lights dimmed as the opening acts were about to perform and Devin walked over to take Kyla by the hand.

"Come join me," he said.

"Sure," she responded.

They went to one side of the suite to listen to the music and talk. The conversation was great; they were hanging on to each other's every word as the chemistry was building. They talked and drank through most of the opening acts and Kyla was beginning to get a bit tipsy so she slowed down; she didn't want to be passed out before Jill Scott came out.

After about an hour, Jill took the stage and it was electrifying. They stood up to dance and sing along with Jill. Devin slipped behind Kyla to place his hands around her waist and rocked back and forth with her. She could feel his hands trailing up and down the small of her back and she was enjoying it. They were bumping and grinding in the dark as if it was only two of them in the room. He slowly leaned in and kissed her neck gently, sending a jolt down her spine. She jumped in shock.

"What are you doing?" she whispered.

"Something I've been wanting to do all night," he responded.

"Kiss my neck?" She said confusingly as she turned to face him.

"Kiss you *anywhere*."

"That was an interesting place to start."

"It was the most accessible. Are you giving me the green light to kiss you anywhere else?"

"Maybe."

With the backdrop of Jill Scott singing, "So Gone," he leaned in and kissed her lips tenderly before she pulled back and stared into his eyes in total silence. The longer they locked eyes, the more she wanted to devour him. She reached up and grabbed the back of his head and kissed him with such passion that he was taken aback.

"Your lips are so soft," he said.

"Yours too."

"They're like perfect little pillows."

Kyla laughed and said, "Nobody has ever described my lips like that before."

"Those were the only words I could think of to describe how they felt on mine."

"Well I hope it was a good feeling."

"It was a great feeling; so much that I want to do it again," he said as kissed her again.

126

As the crowd cheered loudly and Jill took a brief intermission, Kyla could hear someone clearing their throat and looked over to see her sister standing there behind them.

"Jill is killing it," Alexis said, trying to find a reason to get Kyla's attention.

"Yeah, she is," Kyla responded coming out of the lip lock.

Devin glanced over at Alexis in a bit of confusion as to why she was standing over them and asked, "Are you guys enjoying yourselves?"

"Yeah we are and it looks like you guys are too," she said looking over at Kyla for confirmation.

"Indeed, we are," Devin said as they sat down.

"I'm okay, sis," Kyla interjected giving her a thumbs up.

"Okay, carry on," Alexis said as she walked back over to her husband.

"What was that all about?" Devin questioned.

"That's just my sister, she's always been overprotective because I'm the baby."

"Does she think that I'm going to hurt you or something?"

"No but she doesn't want me making any mistakes."

"What mistake would you be making?"

"Moving too fast. I am going through a divorce right now."

"I was going to ask about your wedding ring that is visibly absent. When I saw you in New York, you were quick to tell me that you were engaged and your assistant, well...he was just flat out blocking."

"Yeah, that's Frank. He keeps me together."

"I can see that. What happened with your husband?"

"I don't want to talk about it but let's just say that things didn't work out as planned."

"Damn, that's a shame because he was a lucky guy to have such a beautiful, successful woman like yourself on his arm. If you were mine, I wouldn't let you go."

"You don't really know me. You just know what you see and what I'm presenting to you right now."

"So there is another side to you?"

"There is another side to everybody and people might not like *that* person. For all I know, you might not be who you are presenting yourself to be tonight."

"That's true but there is only one way to find out."

"How is that?"

"By getting to know me."

"I do have a curious question for you though."

"What's that?"

"Why are you single? I mean you could have any woman you want but yet you're rolling around here alone."

"Believe it or not, I'm an introvert and I pour myself into my work and not much else. I've dated plenty of women but none really proved to having staying power."

"What is staying power?"

"They weren't willing to deal with my line of work, the traveling, the late nights and early mornings.

"I can see how that could pose a threat to any relationship. My husband wasn't on board with me working like that either because I keep the same type of schedule as an entertainment attorney. He wanted me to stay home and just have his babies."

"I like your drive for your career, it's part of what makes me attracted to you. You're a go-getter and not to mention you're stunning."

"I appreciate that," she said as Jill reappeared on stage.

They went back to singing and dancing as Jill finished up her show with "Golden," and they all gathered themselves to head backstage to meet Jill as promised. Devin grabbed Kyla's hand as he led her and the others through the crowd to get down and head backstage. He showed his credentials again and they all entered. He introduced them to all of the artists and Kyla was especially excited to meet Jill. They exchanged pleasantries and Kyla told her how much of a fan that she was and how she enjoyed her show. Jill was humble and thanked her for her support. After about twenty minutes backstage Devin offered to walk Kyla to her car because he had to wrap up business at the arena before he could leave. Kyla obliged and hugged her brother-in-law and sister goodnight. They all headed out their separate ways.

Once getting to her car, Devin pulled Kyla into an embrace and asked, "Am I going to see you again?"

"That depends."

"On?"

"Whether or not I have staying power," Kyla said, laughing.

"We'll just have to see about that now won't we," Devin said as he sweetly kissed her goodnight.

"If you keep doing things like that, I might have it," Kyla joked.

"I'll keep that in mind."

"Goodnight and thank you," Kyla said as she got into her car.

"You're welcome and thank you for being my date this evening," Devin said as he shut her door.

Kyla started the car and rolled down the window and with a big smile said, "My pleasure, Mr. Jackson."

"I see we're back to business again."

"Until further notice," Kyla said as she pulled out of the parking space.

The next morning when Kyla came out of her meeting, Frank came into her office with a flower delivery.

"You are having a great week, Ms. Thing," Frank said, as he set the flowers down on her desk.

"I most certainly am," Kyla said with a smile.

"I bet these are from your new *old* boo. They look really expensive too."

"We shall see."

Kyla removed the card from the arrangement and discovered that they were from Devin Jackson so she was hesitant to read the card aloud since he was technically a client of the firm. "These *are* from my old boo. I won't read the card, it's too personal" Kyla responded.

"Okay, I see that Stella has her groove back."

"You are a mess, Frank," Kyla said laughing.

Frank left the office and she carefully read the card.

"Kyla, it was a pleasure spending the evening with you last night and I wanted to send these beautiful flowers to remind you what a beautiful woman you

are and to brighten your day. Hopefully I'll get to find out whether or not you have staying power. DJ."

She took out her phone and sent him a message thanking him for the flowers and he responded, "My pleasure beautiful." This put a smile on her face for the rest of her long work day.

When she finally finished putting in extra hours on a major case, she gathered her things to head home. She got to the house, put her things down and headed upstairs to take a bath in her soaker tub. As she was running the bath water, she heard the doorbell ring. She knew that she wasn't expecting anyone so she considered ignoring it but the bell kept ringing. She went downstairs to see who it could be. To her surprise, she saw Liz standing in front of her door. She didn't want to answer it but she did reluctantly.

Cracking the door, Kyla said, "What are you doing here?"

"Can we talk?" Liz asked.

"I don't have anything to say to you?"

"But I have something to say to you."

"What could you possibly say that I would want to hear?"

"Just let me come in."

"No, you're not welcome in my house. I'll come outside."

"Fair enough."

Kyla came outside onto the steps and shut the door behind her and said, "You have five minutes."

Liz continued, "I know what *I* did was wrong but everything *you* did to Vince was wrong and he deserves better."

"You drove all the way over here to get that off of your chest? You could've sent that in a text or left a voice message."

"I also wanted to drop off the stuff that you left at my house," Liz said as she attempted to hand Kyla a box.

Kyla pushed the box away and said, "You keep it, I don't want anything from you."

"He's never going to take you back."

"Who are you? The judge, jury and executioner?"

"No, but I'm telling you that you brought all of this on yourself."

"Please! Nothing that *I* did in *my* marriage, gave *you* the right to try to sleep with my husband. Your five minutes is up now. You can leave."

"Kyla, as someone who once cared about you deeply, you need to learn to appreciate people and stop taking people for granted. The world does not revolve around you."

"Bye, Liz," Kyla said as she slammed the door in her face and hoping to never see or hear from her again.

Chapter 11

A little over a week has passed since Kyla met with her attorney to respond to Vince's divorce petition. Just as her attorney suspected, they were in for a fight. Vince responded to the petition with counter-offers of his own and things were heating up between them. Their respective attorneys had suggested that they go to mediation to try to work out some of their differences before taking this fight to court. Both were reluctant but agreed to the mediation. In the meantime, they really didn't have too many words to say to each other but Vince's mom once again requested that Melanie come spend the weekend with her. Vince refused to be the go-between so Kyla reluctantly agreed to take her to her grandmother this weekend. She picked Melanie up from the daycare and drove her over to Vince's parents' house. She was hoping to be in and out but, knowing Mrs. Preston, there would be a conversation that could get ugly. Once she arrived at the house, she parked the car and took a deep breath to get herself in the right headspace for a conversation. She took Melanie and the bag out of the car. They walked up to the door to ring the bell but the door opened before she could touch the bell and Mrs. Preston appeared stone faced.

"Well, hello," Mrs. Preston said.

"Hello," Kyla said, to keep it brief.

Melanie reached up for her grandmother to pick her up and Mrs. Preston obliged while saying, "How's grandma's baby? It's about time your mother brought you over here to see me."

Kyla mentally rolled her eyes and said, "Sorry it took me so long to get over here. Work has been crazy lately."

"You work on weekends?" Mrs. Preston said, as she disappeared into the foyer, forcing Kyla to follow her.

"Sometimes."

"Come on in and have a seat."

"I can't stay long; I have plans this evening."

"This won't take long."

Kyla knew where this was about to go so she prepared herself and responded, "Okay."

"Look, this thing between you and Vincent is getting ugly."

"I didn't intend for it to get ugly but..."

Cutting Kyla off, Mrs. Preston asked, "What did you think would happen when you did what you did?"

"With all due respect Mrs. Preston, I don't want to rehash that and besides, your son is not telling you the whole story."

"Well, why don't *you* tell me then?"

"I don't even think it's necessary at this point. If you're worried that I'm going to try to keep Melanie from him, I'm not. He's a great dad and I won't even take that away from him."

"I want to make sure we stay in her life as well and it feels like you've been avoiding us since the breakup."

"I haven't been avoiding you all but I know you had such high hopes for this marriage, as did I, but it didn't turn out the way any of us had planned. I just felt like, if I came around, it would be a constant reminder of what could've been."

"I don't think that either of you tried hard enough to make this work."

"I've never put so much effort into trying to get someone to love me, then I have with your son only to be rejected. I gave up. I simply quit and it's not for the lack of trying. The ball was left in his court and he chose not to shoot it. I just want us to all be cordial and be the best co-parents that Melanie deserves."

"Having your daughter in a healthy environment is important. I don't want all of that fighting around her."

"I'm done fighting."

"Then why are you trying so hard to take him for everything that he has?"

Kyla got up from the table and said, "On that note, Mrs. Preston, I'm leaving. I'll be back for Melanie on Sunday afternoon."

"I wasn't done."

"But I am. Melanie, come give mommy a kiss," Kyla said as she approached the front door.

"I don't like what you are doing to my son," Mrs. Preston said, as Kyla approached her car.

"I don't like that your son slept with my best friend either so I guess that makes two of us that are disappointed," Kyla responded as she got inside of her car and shut the door.

Mrs. Preston stood there, stunned and speechless, before shutting the door and returning to Melanie. Kyla drove off thinking, *"The nerve of that woman trying to chastise me when her son is just as much to blame in all of this as I am."* She raced back into town to meet Frank for a movie and dinner. The two of them saw a romantic comedy and had a much needed laugh to take her mind off of the conversation that she had earlier. They walked out of the theater still laughing and talking about their favorite parts of the movie and in an instant, the laughter came to a screeching halt when Kyla looked through the picture window of the restaurant that they were passing and saw Vince eating dinner with a beautiful woman and they looked really cozy. Kyla stopped dead in her tracks in front of the window.

"What's wrong?" Frank questioned.

"Do you see this?" Kyla responded.

"See what?"

"Look right there in that restaurant," Kyla said, as she pointed in the direction of Vince who couldn't see her.

Frank's eyes got wide and said, "Looks like Vince is on a date."

"Yeah and I'm about to go in there and ruin it," Kyla said, as she started towards the door.

Frank grabbed her by the arm and said, "Don't do that. You have more class than that. You don't want him to see you sweat."

"I do have class so I'm just going to go inside and say hello."

"Somehow I know that's a bad idea but *you're* the boss so I can't stop you."

"That's right. Follow my lead. I want to make that motherfucker uncomfortable."

Frank followed Kyla inside of the restaurant. Together, they went up to the receptionist and asked for a table for two. As the receptionist escorted them away from where Vince and his date were sitting, Kyla asked for the empty table directly across from Vince. The pair sat down and Kyla could see that Vince immediately noticed her.

She turned and looked him straight in his face and then turned back around to Frank and whispered, "He saw us."

"He looks uncomfortable now," Frank whispered back.

"I know," Kyla said with a giggle.

Vince straightened his tie and swallowed hard when he realized that Kyla is sitting beside him. But he didn't lose his cool. He didn't want anyone to cause a scene so he excused himself from his table with Annette and walked over to Kyla's table.

"Let me talk to you for a minute," Vince said, as he leaned in with his back to Annette so she couldn't see anything he was saying.

"About what?" Kyla questioned.

"It's clear that I'm in here with someone and I don't need you acting crazy."

"What makes you think that I care about who you're in here with?"

"I know you and I know how you get with a few drinks."

"I haven't been drinking and I'm also no longer your concern. You threw me out with the trash, remember."

"Let's not do this here."

"Then go back to your little date," Kyla said, with a flick of her wrist.

Vince didn't respond and went back to his own table. When he returned to the table he carried on with business as usual but Annette wasn't buying any of it.

"Who is that?" Annette questioned.

"It's not important," Vince responded.

"Well, she seemed important enough for you to go over there."

135

"If you must know, that's my soon-to-be ex-wife."

"Oh, let me go over there and meet her."

"That's a bad idea."

"Why? She should know the woman who is in your life now."

"It's too soon for that."

"Too soon?"

"Yes, we're still going through this divorce and I don't really need her to have any extra ammunition on top of what she is already trying to use with the lawyers."

"It sounds like she is quite the bitch."

"Don't call her that. You don't even know her."

"Why don't you ever refer to her by name? All of this time that I've been seeing you, you have never once said her name."

"Because that's not important. You don't need to know her name right now and I don't want to talk about her anymore. This night is about you, about us."

"I want to know more about her."

"Why do you keep pressing the issue?"

"Because she is sitting right there and she keeps looking at us."

"I can pay the bill and we can leave if she is making you uncomfortable."

"That's not necessary because we were here first."

"Okay then, let's go back to enjoying ourselves like before she walked in."

Annette finally agreed to drop the conversation about Kyla and meanwhile Kyla and Frank were over there trying to read lips.

"I wonder what they are talking about?" Frank asked.

"I don't know but judging from his body language, he is uncomfortable," Kyla said.

"I think you successfully ruined his date you little evil genius."

"I think I did," Kyla said as she and Frank high fived.

Frank and Kyla watched as Vince and Annette paid their bill and exited the restaurant. On their way out, Vince looked over at Kyla with an evil glance and Kyla returned the favor with a serious side-eye. She was hoping that his date would say something but she didn't. At this point in her life nothing surprised her anymore. Kyla and Frank continued their dinner and then went off to their respective homes.

* * *

It was early Saturday morning and Kyla got up to the clean the house and then work out. Just as she was about to get in the shower she got a call from Sal. Hesitantly, she answered.

"Hello," Kyla said, with a serious lack of enthusiasm.

"Don't sound so happy to hear from me," Sal said.

"You talk about *me* hitting and running. You fell off the planet for two weeks. No call, no text, nothing."

"You're funny."

"How so?"

"You call me to be your 'Maintenance Man', then get upset when I can't be reached. I guess I'm supposed to be on call twenty-four seven for you, huh?"

"Nobody said all of that but when I leave you messages I do expect a response. That's just common courtesy."

"If you must know, I headed out of the country for ten days on vacation and couldn't use my phone."

"Why didn't you tell me when you were here?"

"I didn't think I needed to."

"You know what, I'm trippin, you're absolutely right. You don't owe me anything."

"Are you trying to be funny?"

"No, I'm serious this time. We're just friends and nothing more."

"I understand I missed a chance to go on a hot date with you and Jill Scott. How was the show?"

"The show was great. Jill was..." Kyla said, as she got cut off by the call waiting on her cellphone.

"I didn't hear you," Sal said.

"Hold on, I got another call," Kyla said, as she switched to the other line to say hello.

"Hello, beautiful," Devin said.

"Hello, Mr. Jackson," Kyla responded.

"What are you up to right now?"

"Hold on a second, I have to get rid of the other call I was on," Kyla said before returning to Sal.

"Now, what were you saying?" Sal asked.

"Let me call you back, I need to take this call," Kyla responded.

"Okay."

Once Sal hung up, she returned to Devin.

"I'm back, now where were we Mr. Jackson?"

"We were at me asking you to get dressed and accompany me to the Hamptons for the day. I have to attend an event there."

"The Hamptons? Just for the day?"

"If it gets too late, we can stay, but I promise to be the perfect gentleman."

"Okay what do I need to wear and when do I need to be ready?"

"It's an all-white affair and I need you ready by 2:00PM. I will be there to get you."

"Great, I'll be ready and I'll text you my address."

"See you then."

Kyla hopped in the shower and pulled a bunch of dresses out of her closet to see which one she would look the best in before settling on a form-fitting pencil skirt with a bustier top and gold Giuseppe Zanotti sling backs with a gold Gucci clutch bag. She packed an overnight bag just in case they didn't return. Once she got dressed with hair and makeup done, she went down to the living room to wait for Devin. When she heard the doorbell ring, she did one last mirror check and headed for the door. When she pulled the door open Devin was standing there in a white tailored linen suit that gave his sun kissed skin an extra glow. He flashed a big smile when he saw her and held out his hand for her to join him. She carefully stepped outside and he opened the door to the black Bentley Phantom parked in her driveway. They got into the back seat and the driver took off, headed to New York. After the three-hour drive, they arrived at a sprawling waterfront mansion, parked, and went inside. Kyla looked around in awe at all of the marble and beautiful décor.

"Where is everyone?" Kyla asked.

"This isn't where the party is, it's one of my summer properties," Devin responded.

"*One* of them?"

"I like to have options."

"I can see that. This is beautiful."

"Thank you. I'm usually too busy working to enjoy it so I use it as mostly rental property but I knew that I was coming up here for the event so I made sure that it was free and clear because I know you are a private person."

"That I am."

"Would you like anything, Madame?" A man's voice said behind Kyla.

Kyla turned around and said, "What are my options?"

"Whatever you'd like," Devin responded.

"I'll just have water for now," Kyla said.

"Sparkling?" the butler asked.

"That's fine," she responded.

"You can relax; the party isn't until 8:00PM so we have plenty of time."

"I want to go sit outside and watch the waves. That seems so relaxing. I don't get much time to do that."

"Relaxation is important, even though I don't get much of it myself. Perhaps I will join you out on the deck."

The two went out on the deck and just sat there together watching the sun set and the listening to the waves crashing against the rocks. It all seemed so surreal to Kyla. Her life seemed to be taking a turn for the better but she didn't want to get ahead of herself. He seemed too good to be true. After a few minutes of silence, he asked her to come sit with him on the oversized plush lounge chair so she got up and moved over to where he was and she sat down between his legs and leaned back onto his chest as he wrapped his arm around the front of her.

"I haven't felt this relaxed in a while," Kyla said.

"I'm glad that you could relax a bit," Devin said as he leaned in to kiss her on the cheek.

With a smile on her face, Kyla turned her head toward Devin and kissed him gently on the lips. Before long, they were in a full on lip lock and Devin stopped before they got too far to turn back.

"We better get ready. I am going to have Peter touch up my suit, do you want anything?" Devin asked.

"No, my clothing is stretchy so it doesn't wrinkle but I am going to touch up my make-up a bit," Kyla responded.

"I will show you to the guest room if you prefer."

"That would be nice."

Devin walked her down the hall to what some would consider an apartment. He showed her where everything was and told her that he would be right down the hall in the master suite. She went inside the huge bathroom and touched up her hair and makeup. After about fifteen minutes, she ventured down the hall to where Devin said he would be and just before she was about to knock, the door swung open and he was standing there in nothing but boxer briefs. His skin so perfect with tattooed sleeves on both arms, washboard abs and a bulging package to top it all off. He was immediately surprised to see Kyla standing at the door because he was expecting his butler Peter.

"I'm so sorry," Kyla said as her cheeks turned red with embarrassment.

"It's okay, I wasn't expecting to run into you either but I'm sure you've seen men in underwear before."

"I have but it was purposeful. I'm going to wait downstairs."

"It's okay, you can come in. I won't bite, I promise. You can have a seat on the bed."

"Are you sure? This is a bit awkward seeing you like this?"

"Why?

"Because I'm your attorney."

"Not tonight. Tonight you're my date and we're not going to discuss business when we're together anymore, unless it pertains to my *actual* business. We can keep things professional when we need to because we're both adults capable of making the switch when necessary."

"I guess you *told* me."

"I want you to be feel comfortable around me and not worried about breaking your business and pleasure rule. Right now, this is all pleasure."

"I got it."

There was a knock at the door and it was Peter returning with Devin's freshly pressed suit. He handed it to him and he slipped it on as Kyla watched his every move, imagining what it must feel like to be that suit lying strategically on every muscle of his body. She knew full well she wasn't going to do anything sexual with him at this point but it was great imagery.

Once he was dressed, he reached for her hand to help her up from the bed and wrapped her arm around his bicep as they headed downstairs to the car. The driver took them about a mile down the road to yet another mansion but this time it was filled with a ton of people, inside and out. The music was loud and this clearly looked like an industry party. They walked around shaking hands as she was being introduced to several people. She was in her element and thought about picking up some new clients while she was here but remembered that he told her this was about pleasure and not business. They danced and drank the evening away before returning back to his place around 1:00AM. They were both tipsy and tired, so going back to Pennsylvania was not going to be an option. Devin escorted Kyla upstairs to the guest room and gave her a long lingering kiss goodnight before heading down the hall to his room. She got undressed to take a shower and when she was done she put on a pair of small shorts and a little t-shirt before heading to bed. Just as she was about to slip under the covers she heard a knock at the door.

"Are you decent?" Devin said.

"Sure, you can come in," Kyla said.

Devin entered the room wearing basketball shorts and a white tank top. He sat down on the bed beside her and asked, "Did you enjoy yourself tonight?"

"I did. I had a great time, thank you again."

"You're welcome. I just wanted to see if you needed anything before I went back to my room."

"No, I'm okay."

"I do need something from you though, if you don't mind."

"What's that?"

"To come lay with me."

"Just lay?"

"Yes, I just want to lie next to you. When we were together earlier it felt really good."

"Okay, I think I can do that. To be clear, we're just laying together right?"

Devin laughed and said, "Yes, unless you have other plans."

"No, I just wanted to be sure."

Kyla got up from the bed and walked down the hall with Devin to his room. His room was facing the ocean and he had all of the windows open so that they could feel the ocean breeze and hear the waves crashing against the rocks. It was very dark out there but peaceful. She crawled onto the massive bed and curled up next to him as he put his arms around her, kissed her on the shoulder softly as they listened to the sound of the waves together and fell off to sleep. As promised, he was the perfect gentleman.

The next morning Kyla crawled out of bed while Devin was still asleep and headed down the hall to the guest room to brush her teeth and wash her face. While she was freshening up, Peter knocked at the door.

"Madame, Mr. Jackson has asked me to bring you breakfast but he didn't know what you ate so I wanted to ask you what you wanted."

"Oh, that's sweet. I will take an egg white omelet with spinach, peppers and onions. I'll also take some wheat toast and coffee."

"Cream and sugar?"

"Yes."

"Where should I bring it?"

"You can bring it to Mr. Johnson's room when you bring his food."

"Okay."

Kyla went back down the hall and climbed back onto the bed with Devin, which caused him to awaken when he felt the movement.

"Good morning, beautiful. How did you sleep?" Devin asked.

"I slept good," Kyla responded.

"I hope you don't mind but I told Peter to bring us breakfast in bed but he was supposed to check with you before he started cooking."

"I ran into Peter in the hallway a little while ago and he asked me what I wanted."

"Great."

"You know, I really underestimated you."

"How so?"

"I had a preconceived notion about guys like you but you are slowly but surely proving me wrong."

"What do you mean by guys like me?"

"Guys who are attractive successful business men. From past experiences, men like you tend to mistreat women because you get what you want, when you want."

"I'm not sure what type of guys that you are used to dealing with but I was raised to respect women, treat them like queens, and value them. I'd like to think that I'm a good guy, despite having had some bad relationships in the past."

"From what I can tell, you are a good guy but it's still early yet."

"Yes, it is and from what I can tell, you are worth my time until you show me otherwise."

"That's good to know."

"Do you want to watch TV?"

"Sure."

Devin reached for the remote and turned on the flat screen television mounted on the wall in front of them. He handed her the remote and told her that she could watch whatever she wanted while he got up and went to the bathroom. She lay there flipping through channels before settling on Law and Order SVU reruns. Once there was a commercial, she got up and walked towards the door of the large wrap-around balcony, opened it and headed outside. She headed toward the railing that was facing the ocean and leaned over to watch the water. She closed her eyes and inhaled the fresh air and sounds of nature before a pair of hands slipping around her waist startled her.

"Did I scare you?" Devin asked.

"A little bit," Kyla responded.

"I'm sorry but I couldn't resist."

"It seems that you like to touch."

"I'm guilty. I do like to touch, but with permission though," he said as he put his hands in the air.

"I don't mind. I give you permission to touch me."

"Do I have your permission to kiss you?"

"You don't need permission; you've already cleared that hurdle."

"Great," he said, as he turned her around and placed his lips on hers.

They were kissing for what felt like an eternity and they were beginning to get to a point where things could go further. They walked back inside of the bedroom still in a lip lock as he laid her gently onto the bed. Just as the line was about to be crossed, Peter knocked on the door with the food delivery and they shuffled to get side by side on the bed.

"Mr. Johnson, your food is ready sir," Peter said through the door.

"You can bring it in," Devin said, as he pulled the covers up over his waist to hide the fact that he had an erection.

Kyla took a deep breath and was actually happy that Peter came just in time before they went too far. He came in and sat the trays down on the bed. They ate breakfast and then got dressed to travel back to the city. They cuddled up in the car and stole a few kisses but most of all they got to know each other a little more and it was clear that a relationship was budding. After the three-hour journey, Kyla made it home and Devin walked her to the door, kissed her goodbye, and she went inside with a smile. She had a great weekend but she dreaded returning to the Preston residence to pick up Melanie. She put her stuff down and headed back out to go get Melanie.

When Kyla arrived at the Preston residence, she noticed Vince's car parked in the driveway and right away she wanted to put her car in reverse to avoid whatever set up was going on inside. She parked the car, got out, and headed to the door but she could hear them out back so she walked around the side and entered the yard.

"Hello," Kyla said, waving to everyone in the yard.

"Hi," Mrs. Preston said.

"What's up," Vince said with a head nod.

"Is that a hello?" Kyla questioned.

"Isn't that the meaning of what's up?" Vince responded.

"I don't have time to play your games. Where is my baby?"

"She's inside sleeping."

"Well can you go get her?"

"Can you tell me why you told my mom I slept with Liz?"

"Can you tell your mom why you did it?"

"I didn't sleep with her."

"So she lied?"

"Yeah."

"Whatever."

"I'm going to get my daughter."

"I think you're being unreasonable asking for all of that stuff in the divorce."

"I think you're being unreasonable thinking that I don't deserve it."

"You don't."

"We'll let the judge decide that. See you next week at the mediation."

"Why are you doing this?"

"You should ask yourself, why you wanted a divorce. I'm giving you what you want, so you can go on with your life. I wouldn't want to keep you from being happy," Kyla said, as she entered the house to go get Melanie. She scooped her sleeping body up off of the couch and picked up her bag that was by the door and headed to her car. She strapped Melanie in her car seat and drove off without saying goodbye to anybody.

Chapter 12

The day had finally come for Vince and Kyla to face off with the help of a mediator. Vince woke up earlier than usual feeling a wide range of emotions. He never imagined that their marriage could have gotten so out of control. He wasn't sure what he was about to walk into but if the twists and turns over the last few years were any indicator; he knew things were about to get crazier. Months ago, when Vince decided on the divorce, he thought the process would be quick and easy. Through all the years, one thing remained constant, nothing was ever quick and easy with Kyla. Nonetheless, Vince was ready for the battle.

He took a shower, put on one of his famous power suits and headed out the door to the mediator's office. When he arrived, Kyla was already waiting and since she was early, it wasn't a good sign considering she ran late for everything so this meant she had a strategy prepared. He walked into the conference room, where Kyla was already seated at the head of a large wooden table with the mediator seated in the center. The mediator advised Vince to sit across from Kyla to keep the lines of communication open.

"I'd like to first thank you both for coming and agreeing to mediation in lieu of court. My name is Sandra James and I will be your mediator throughout this process. Let me begin by explaining how divorce mediation works. I don't work for either party so I will be neutral throughout the negotiation process. We are here to open the lines of communication between the two of you to make things as amicable as possible when the marriage is over. Each party will be given a chance to speak on a given issue. The goal is to walk away with agreements that both parties are satisfied with. It could be one or many sessions to reach a consensus between the two of you. We want to stick to the issues and steer clear of personal attacks. If we are unable to reach any agreement or if it becomes too contentious, we will cease the mediation and recommend you go back to your respective legal counsel for next steps."

They both nodded their head in agreement as she continued, "Are we ready to get started?"

"Yes," Kyla said first.

"Yes," Vince said following Kyla's lead.

"Let's start with the first issue. Mrs. Preston, you are asking for the house, which means you want Mr. Preston to continue to pay half of the mortgage and Mr. Preston, you think the property should be sold and the assets split between the two of you or for her to buy you out of your portion. Mrs. Preston, why do you think you should keep the house?"

"I should get the house because it is our first family home. We bought the house together and wanted to make a life together but he chose to walk out on that but that shouldn't mean he gets to walk out on his responsibility to pay for the home that he chose to leave."

"Mr. Preston, any response?"

"I didn't chose to leave, she pushed me out the door when she decided to have an affair. I don't think I should keep paying for a house that I am never going to live in while she does whatever she wants, with whomever she wants in it. I'm not doing that so we need to sell it or she can buy me out, plain and simple."

"You can afford it," Kyla interjected.

"That's not the point," Vince responded.

"Our daughter shouldn't have to be ripped away from her home because you're being petty," Kyla said.

"I'm not being petty, I'm being real and you won't get a dime from me towards that house. Our daughter will be fine in another house that *you* buy," Vince said.

"We'll see about that," Kyla snapped.

"Mr. and Mrs. Preston, let's calm down. It doesn't seem like we're going to agree on the house issue today but now that we are clear as to what the stance is on the house, perhaps you all can consider a compromise for the next time that we come together to discuss this. Let's move on to the custody issue. Mrs. Preston, you are asking for full custody and child support. Mr. Preston, you want joint custody and no support. Mr. Preston, let's start with you on the custody issue."

147

"I want joint custody of my daughter, period end of story."

"Can you talk more about why you think joint custody is the best option?" Ms. James asked.

"I don't think Kyla is fit to be a full-time mom. Her job is very demanding, she travels often and she has started drinking a lot more lately. I think my daughter needs to be me with just as much or if not more than her."

"That's bullshit Vince and you know it," Kyla yelled.

"Calm down Mrs. Preston, you'll get your turn. Are you done, Mr. Preston?"

"Yes."

"Now, Mrs. Preston, you can talk about why you are seeking full custody."

"For the same damn reason he just said. He just got a new role at his job that is going to have him traveling more. His mother hates me so I don't know what the hell she might be telling my daughter since he'll have Melanie with her most of the time when he is too busy. He walked out on this family and now he has some new little tramp that he is running around town with so how much time will he really have to spend with a toddler?"

"Well now, that was a mouth full. Any rebuttal to that Mr. Preston?" Ms. James asked.

"Yes, there is actually. Where the hell do you get off talking about my mother putting things in our daughter's head? She would never do that so I think you went too far with that. I know that you aren't suggesting that I would put a woman over our daughter. I would never do that and you know it so I resent that fact that you even used that."

"I don't know what you might do anymore. I thought I knew you but evidently I don't"

"The same could be said about you."

"I never thought that you would question the paternity of our daughter but you did."

"I never thought that you would cheat on me but you did."

"I never cheated on you during this marriage and if you would have just fucking listened to me the million times I tried to tell you that, you would know that but instead you chose to cheated on *me* and with my best friend at that."

148

"Okay, it's never good to bring up hurt during these mediations. It doesn't lend itself to healthy dialogue. Let me remind you again that we need to stick only to the issues," Ms. James interrupted.

"You know what, I need a break. This is giving me a headache," Kyla said as she stood up to excuse herself from the table.

"Okay, let's take a few minutes to collect ourselves and I'll see you guys back here in ten minutes," Ms. James said.

"Thank you," Kyla said, as she left the conference room.

She walked into the hallway and broke down in tears. She thought that she was strong and able to handle to the mediation, but it was too much to sit face-to-face with the man that she still loved while they spewed vitriol at each other. She knew that even though she was hurt by what he did with Liz; she wasn't ready to walk away but her hand was forced. Even with all of the fun in the past few weeks with Devin and Sal, she couldn't help that she was still in love with the man in that room who sat across from her today. The realization that this was the beginning of the end just wasn't sitting right with her. While Kyla readied herself by wiping away her tears, Vince grabbed her, wiped the falling tears from her eyes and pulled her into a silent embrace. They were both struggling and as odd as it seemed, they needed each other's strength in that moment. Kyla broke the embrace and headed back inside and Vince followed.

"Okay, are you all ready to continue?" Ms. James said.

"Actually, I think I need a little more time," Vince said, to everyone's surprise.

"Do you need a longer recess?" Ms. James asked.

"No, I think I want to call it a day and we can come back another day."

"I see. Mrs. Preston, are you okay with coming back for another session?"

"Sure."

"In that case, you can make another appointment when you both can agree on your schedules."

"Sounds good," Vince said.

"I look forward to our next session," Ms. James said, as everyone stood up to shake hands.

Both Vince and Kyla headed out of the conference room and onto the elevator where they took the quiet ride together. They went their separate ways in the lobby and headed off to work both mentally and emotionally drained.

* * *

A few weeks went by since Vince and Kyla had their mediation. Summer was coming to a close and it couldn't come fast enough for Kyla. Things were still pretty unsettled but they mustered up enough forgiveness to throw Melanie a first birthday party. It wasn't the over-the-top lavish affair that Kyla wanted but she was willing to compromise with Vince to scale it back. They hosted the party in the backyard, and decorated the house in a princess theme. There was a moon bounce and face painting for the kids and both Kyla and Melanie were dressed in little pink tutus for the occasion. The house was filled with friends and family, including both sets of parents and siblings. Kyla's brother Winston had even flown in from North Carolina for the party. For the moment, everyone appeared to be happy and Kyla was even getting along with Mrs. Preston.

Kyla and Vince took several family photos with Melanie and it felt like old times. In one of the pictures the photographer asked them to hold Melanie and each kiss her on the cheek and as they were setting up the picture and holding Melanie, she moved her head forward and they accidently kissed each other as Melanie clapped with excitement. Although it was purely accidental, it was a sweet moment and they both knew it. They finished taking photos and went around the party mingling and talking to people, many of whom had no idea that they were even getting divorced.

"You two look like you're getting along," Alexis said.

"For the moment," Kyla responded.

"That's good. We can't have everyone in your business you know."

"Yeah, tell me about it. People are very nosey."

"So what's up with Mr. Music Producer?"

"You mean Mr. CEO? He's good."

"You still seeing him?"

"Yeah we're still seeing each other but nothing too serious."

"I couldn't tell it wasn't getting serious from the concert. He seems to be totally into you."

"You're funny. We're taking it slow. He's really a great guy too but..."

"But what?"

"I don't know if I'm ready to move on."

"What do you mean? You're moving on. Divorce remember?"

"I know but this divorce is doing something to me."

"Like what?"

"I thought I was over Vince but I don't think that I am."

"You're not going to be over him that fast but you said yourself that he has moved on."

"I don't know if he's moved on but he *was* on a date and that doesn't necessarily mean anything."

"Don't sell yourself short. He's out here dating so you owe it to yourself to see what this new guy is all about. Right bro?" Alexis said, as their brother Winston walked up on the tail end of her sentence.

"I don't know what you're talking about but sure," he said laughing.

"I was just telling little sis to keep her options open that's all," Alexis said.

"Personally I think you and Vince should work it out because that's my man. I like that dude," Winston said.

"Focus Winston, he's divorcing her remember?" Alexis said.

"I can't tell by the way that he keeps looking at you with adoration," Winston pointed out.

"Really?" Kyla asked.

"Seriously. Look," Winston said.

Kyla carefully glanced over at Vince only to see him looking at her with a smile on his face. She hadn't seen that in months but she didn't want to get her hopes up because he could just be pretending for the moment.

"When are *you* going to settle down yourself?" Kyla asked.

"You ask me that every time I come home," Winston responded.

"That's because you have been avoiding marriage like the plague," Alexis said.

"I haven't been avoiding it, I'm just not ready yet. I do have a new girl though and it's getting pretty serious."

"You always have a new girl," Kyla said.

"And you always claim it's serious," Alexis said.

"I like to have options, what do you want me to say," Winston said laughing.

"At some point you need to go with one option and stick with it," Alexis said.

"Didn't you hear the man, he said this one is serious," Kyla said.

"Serious my ass," Alexis responded.

Kyla and her siblings laughed and talked a little while longer before it was time to sing happy birthday and cut the cake. They summoned everyone, gathered around the cake and sang to Melanie as she tried to grab the cake off of the table throughout the song. Vince and Kyla helped her blow out the candle and let her snatch the first piece of cake off the side of the cake. Once the singing was done, they opened up all of the gifts. The party went on a little while longer and everyone cleared out leaving a mess. Vince stayed behind to help Kyla clean up the house and put away all of the gifts. When they were done, they got Melanie ready for bed and put her down for the night. Once she was tucked in they went into the family room and sat down on the couch. Kyla sat next to Vince and he put his arm around her and they talked about Melanie as two proud parents would do. After, they turned on the television, and before long, the television was watching them. They had fallen asleep on the couch together in a spooning position and by the time Vince had awakened the sun was rising. Vince got up and attempted to slip out of the back door but before he was fully outside, he turned back to see Kyla one last time, sleeping peacefully before he continued to his car. The sound of the door closing caused Kyla to wake up and realize that Vince had left. This seemed to be their narrative. Every time she looked around, he was gone.

* * *

A few days after Melanie's party Annette came over to Vince's apartment after work. Since the mediation began, Vince had been acting a bit out of character and it was starting to concern Annette. Vince rushed home, to the dinner that she prepared for him. Vince was noticeably quiet so Annette started asking him questions to get him talking because he didn't seem to be his normal jovial and attentive self.

"Babe, how was work today?" she asked.

"It was okay, nothing spectacular. How was your day?" he responded.

"Just another day at the office I guess,"

"That's good," he responded as if he didn't really care.

"You never told me how your daughter's party was."

"It was great. She had a good time with her family."

"I wish I could've been there with you to celebrate the little lady."

"You know why you couldn't go right?"

"I know but I guess I'm kind of wondering when will be the right time."

"These things take time. You have to know this since *your* divorce was just final."

"I'm not talking about the divorce; I'm talking about letting your ex know about me so that she is comfortable with me around Melanie."

"She will find out about you in due time. She's very protective of Melanie so I don't know when she'll be comfortable with you around her but we'll work up to that."

"I just hate that I can't see you whenever Melanie's around."

"That's my daughter and I have to do what's best for her."

"I get it but I just wish it could be different and that your ex would understand that you have moved on and it's always a possibility that another woman might be around her daughter."

"Can we talk about something else?"

"Why do we always have to change the subject when we start talking about her?"

"Because we don't need to talk about her."

"I feel like we can't talk about *us* until we talk about *her*."

"Then let's not."

"Let's not what?"

"Talk about us if it bothers you that much."

"You don't have to be like that."

"I do because I'm dealing with a lot with this divorce and you don't seem to care and right now you're making it about *your* feelings."

"I do care. I care about you a lot and I want you to be happy—but I also don't want to feel like you have to keep me a secret."

"I'm not trying to keep you a secret but when you have custody agreements and spousal support being thrown in your face by someone who is an attorney, you must tread lightly."

"You never told me she was an attorney."

"I didn't need to."

"That's the first thing you ever told me about her."

"And even that is too much information."

"What do you think I might do with that information? Do you think I'm going to do something to her?"

"It's not what I think *you* might do to *her*, it's the other way around and the less you know about her the better. Trust me."

"I'm not afraid of her if that's what you think."

"I didn't say that you had to be but like I said, we don't need to discuss her any further."

"Okay," Annette said, as she folded her arms and flopped back on the couch in a form of protest.

Vince leaned over and grabbed her and kissed her to get her mind off of Kyla. She smiled and kissed him back and tried to coax him into sex but his unresponsiveness to her advances made her give up. They went on to watch television before going to bed. Vince lay gazing up at the ceiling feeling unsettled about his conversation with Annette. He finally dozed off to sleep after trying to clear this head for an hour-and-a-half.

* * *

Kyla was wrapping up her work day when her office phone rang. It was Frank.

"Devin Jackson is on the line. Would you like me to take a message since you're on your way out?" Frank asked.

"No, put him through," Kyla responded.

"Okay."

In an instant, Devin was on the line.

"Kyla Preston," she said.

"Hello Mrs. Preston, it's Devin Jackson."

"Hello Mr. Jackson, how can I help you?"

"I am in need of your legal expertise."

"That's why I'm your attorney. What can I help you with?"

"I have a contract that needs reviewing but it's short notice. Are you available this evening, maybe over dinner?"

"I have to pick up my daughter but I can see if her dad can pick her up for me. Can I get right back to you? Are you at the office?"

"Yes, you can reach me here."

"Okay, I will call you back."

Kyla hung up to call Vince; he agreed to pick up Melanie from the daycare. She called Devin back and agreed to meet up with him for dinner. She grabbed her brief case to head out the door.

Devin was waiting for her outside of the restaurant as she handed her keys to the valet. As they sat down, Kyla was careful to look around to see if she saw anyone from the firm. This was the first time they'd been out in a public setting together since they started seeing each other. Kyla nervously placed the napkin in her lap as the server poured them sparkling water and took their drink orders.

"This place is nice. I don't think I've ever eaten here before," Kyla said, as she looked around in admiration.

"It is and it's quiet and secluded, which is why I come here," Devin responded, as he grabbed her hand from across the table.

"Devin, I'm really glad that you called me because there is something that I wanted to talk to you about," Kyla said.

"Before we get into the pleasure let's start with the business," Devin said, as he reached down for the contracts in his briefcase.

"Oh, you were serious. I thought you were using that as a cover for calling me at the office to ask me to dinner."

"No, I call the office for business and your cell phone for pleasure. See how I am able to draw that line?"

"I see. Well what do you have here?"

"I have been in talks with a really good friend in LA who was looking to merge his company with mine because he doesn't have the financial means to support it any longer without outside help. I've asked him to draw up a contract and told him I'd have my attorney review it to see if it was smart business. We have to move quickly on it, he is losing the building in a few days and it's prime real estate so I'd like to save it if I can."

"Okay, let me review the terms of the merger," Kyla said as she studied the papers.

She looked through the numbers line-by-line terms before asking questions. Once she was done she said, "This looks more like an acquisition rather than a merger."

"How so?"

"Based on these terms you are simply acquiring his company and all of his debt but he still gets to retain his staff, title and controlling interest in his share of the company. My suggestion would be to change the terms so that if you are acquiring the company and all of the debt, you are the sole owner of the company with all of the controlling interest and appoint him as chairman of a division of the company. How lucrative would this deal really be for you?"

"It would be a huge opportunity for Chess Entertainment to expand into LA and open up some other business ventures for me as well."

"How will you manage a company in LA from here?"

"I would have to actually relocate temporarily to LA to get this off the ground the way that it needs to be. My Philadelphia operation is running like a well-oiled machine and I have a person in place that can run it when I'm not here. I'll be coming back and forth."

"So where does that—," Kyla stopped mid-sentence.

"Where does what?" Devin questioned.

"Nothing."

"Will you re-write the terms and get them back to my office tomorrow?"

"I can do that and my assistant will be sure to send you the bill," Kyla said with a smile.

"I'm never late with my payments."

"And we appreciate that."

"Now let's skip to the pleasure part of this meeting."

"Okay,"

"I was thinking you could come to LA with me for a few days to look at houses."

"When?"

"As soon as this deal is done. I want to get out there quickly."

"I don't think I can just pick up and leave on such short notice. I do have a job and a one-year old to consider."

"You're right. How about I pick a definitive date so that you could make arrangements for your daughter or better yet, you can bring her too."

"I don't think bringing her would be a good idea."

"Why not?"

"Her dad wouldn't be comfortable with that."

"I will hire you a nanny to take care of her if that's your concern."

"That's not what he would be worried about. It would be another man that he hasn't met or that I barely know on a personal level, spending time with her and in another state no less."

"If you want, I could meet him if that would make you feel better."

Kyla nearly choked on her water before saying, "I'll let you know."

"Is this going to be a problem for us?"

"What?"

"My move to LA?"

"Actually I think it is. I don't know if I'm built for a long distance courtship."

"I thought you had staying power?"

"I do but we are just getting to know each other and developing a relationship but I don't know if that is possible if you are on another coast most of the time."

"It's only going to be temporary until the company is up and running and you know I have the means to fly you in, whenever you want."

"I don't want to make any promises so let's take this one day at a time and see how it goes."

"I can do that."

They finished dinner and Kyla was both relieved and disappointed. She was going to tell him that she wanted to slow things down until her divorce was final but he beat her to it with the news of moving to LA. She wanted the opportunity to get to know him better and see where things could go once she was finally free and decidedly over Vince but there was no way she could do that in a bi-coastal relationship. She also didn't want to come across as yet another woman who didn't want to deal with his nomadic behavior but she had to consider her career and daughter in the equation. Her fairytale relationship seemed like it was coming to an end. Devin walked Kyla out, paid for her valet and kissed her good night. She headed home with the contracts and a lot to consider.

When she reached home, she poured a glass of wine and got right to work on the contract. As she worked, she thought about how much she was starting to fall for him and thought about taking him up on his offer to visit LA to see if she really did have staying power. She figured she could work the trip in as a part of the contract, which would allow her to travel on business. She decided to give Devin a call. After a few rings he picked up.

"Hey beautiful. You miss me already?" Devin joked.

"You're funny. I was thinking about the LA offer. Once the contract meets your approval, maybe I can accompany you to make sure that everything goes smoothly. We can travel on business and I can stay for a few days to help you search for a place. How does that sound?" Kyla asked.

"I like the sound of that. If we fly out on Monday will that give you enough time to make arrangements for your daughter?"

"Yes, but I'll need to be back on a red-eye by Thursday."

"Great, I'll make the arrangements."

"The firm will pay for my accommodations with *your* money of course."

"Why can't you stay with me?"

"We're going on business but maybe we'll have an overnight meeting in *my* room."

"Would you let me stay with you?"

"If you promise to be a gentleman."

"I'm always a gentleman but *you* have to promise to keep your hands to yourself."

"I'm a lady, why wouldn't I?" Kyla asked jokingly.

"And *that* you are. So I will see you tomorrow when I come by to pick up the contracts."

"Great."

Kyla hung up with Devin and reluctantly made arrangements with Vince to keep Melanie for a few days so that she could take the trip. She had to be careful with the custody issue looming over her head. She was disappointed that she had to toe the line with work and her personal life to keep him from trying to take her daughter as he promised in the mediation.

* * *

It was early Monday morning and the sun had yet to rise. Kyla rushed around the house in the dark trying to ensure that she wasn't leaving anything behind. Although she was only going to be gone for three days, she packed for twelve. She packed extra because she could never be too sure with Devin who was always full of surprises. Just as she took one last look around the house, she heard the doorbell ring. Quickly, she switched on a few lamps and the porch light to give off the appearance that someone was home as she headed to the door. It was Devin's driver who offered to take her bags as she locked up and went to the car. Once she got in, she saw Devin with a big beaming smile. He leaned in, gave her a quick kiss and told her how beautiful she looked as he grabbed her hand.

"How long did you say you were staying?" Devin asked, studying the endless parade of bags going in the truck of the car.

"I couldn't decide what to pack," Kyla said laughing.

"So you packed your entire closet?"

"No, I packed for all of your surprises."

"What if I told you that you didn't need to pack any clothes?"

"It's too late for that but I'm curious. Why wouldn't I need to pack?"

"I can buy you whatever you need when we get there."

"I couldn't ask you to do that."

"You wouldn't have to ask."

"That's good to know because I love a man who can take charge. There is something sexy about that."

"There is something sexy about a strong business woman," Devin said as he leaned in to steal another kiss.

They pulled up to the airport as the car made its way through a back entrance off the beaten path. Kyla was confused because she'd never been to this part of the airport. The car started towards a hanger and then she realized that they were taking a private plane as they pulled up next to a beautiful small luxury jet.

"You have your own plane?" Kyla asked curiously.

"Not exactly, but I do have a flight company that I use for long flights so that I can be comfortable and today, I want you to be comfortable," Devin responded.

"This is the first time a client has flown me on a private jet."

"Like I said before, I want you to be comfortable and I appreciate you for making the trip with me."

"I appreciate you for bringing me."

"Well you *are* getting paid," Devin said laughing.

"And you're getting a new office and possibly a new house."

The driver removed the luggage and started handing it to the flight crew. The pilot greeted Devin and Kyla and introduced them to the crew.

As they boarded the plane, Kyla looked around at the leather seating, crystal stemware and stocked bar. She thought to herself that she could get used to living like this. They settled in on two seats in the center of the aircraft and next to one another, with Kyla by the window so she could watch the skyline. After the pilot made a few announcements, they were off in the air. She curled up next to Devin with a blanket and took a nap. The two slept about an hour and woke up to strategize over breakfast until the flight landed. Once they landed in LA, a car was waiting to take them to the Beverly Wilshire Hotel. Upon arrival, they requested adjoining rooms in the Beverly wing on the top floor to take in the beautiful views of the LA skyline. Once settled in, they prepared for the 10:00AM meeting. They headed to an office building just a short drive down Wilshire Blvd. Once inside, they found their way to the third floor, where the meeting would take place. As the two entered the glass double doors, Kyla's phone rang from a Philadelphia number so she decided to answer.

"You go ahead," she told Devin as she stayed outside in the hallway.

"Hello," Kyla answered.

"Mrs. Preston?" said the voice on the other end.

"Yes, this is Mrs. Preston."

"Hi, this is Ms. Michelle from Future Scholars Childcare Center."

"Hi, is everything okay?"

"Melanie has been lethargic and is running a pretty high fever so we were calling to see if you could come and pick her up. Our policy is to send children home when they are sick, as to not infect the other children and staff. She'll also have to stay home until she is fever free for 48 hours."

"Ms. Michelle, I'm out of town on business. I'll have to call her dad to see if he can come and pick her up."

"We've tried calling him earlier but we were unable to reach him at the office, does he have another number we can try?"

"I will try him on his cell phone and get back to you. If I can't reach him, I will have another family member there to pick her up. Thank you for calling."

"Thank you and I look to hearing from you soon."

"Sure thing."

Kyla hung up the phone and called Vince on his cell but the phone went to voicemail. She tried him again but was still unsuccessful so she decided to call Alexis.

"What's up sis?"

"Hey, I need you to do me a favor."

"What do you need?"

"The daycare just called and said that Melanie is sick and running a high fever. I can't get a hold of Vince so can you go and pick her up."

"Sure, where should I take her?"

"Can you get take her to your house until I can get a hold of Vince?"

"Yeah I can do that but where are you?"

"I'm in LA on business."

"Okay, I'm leaving my job now."

"Thanks sis. Love you."

"Love you, too."

Kyla called the daycare to inform them that her sister was on the way. She also left Vince a voicemail letting him know where Melanie was and what happened. She got herself together and went back into the meeting. Worried about Melanie, she was a bit off of her game. She found Devin and two other gentlemen in the conference room laughing and engaged in casual conversation. She took a seat next to Devin as he introduced herself.

"This is my attorney Kyla Preston," Devin said.

"Pleased to meet you, I'm Chris Banks, and this is my attorney, Kevin Gray."

"Likewise," Kyla said.

Kyla shook hands and wasted no time getting straight down to business. She pulled out the contracts and detailed the terms of the acquisition. Since Mr. Banks had little to bring to the table, there were very little negotiations by way of counter offers. The only thing that he wanted in the deal was to head a division of the LA offices of Chess Entertainment once it was up and running. Devin agreed to that with the stipulation that he got to choose the division that would be the right fit for him and that Chris would sign a two-year non-compete clause that prevented him from starting a new label. After the two shook hands, they signed the deal and Devin got on the phone to do a wire-transfer of the funds. Once the deal was finalized, Devin and Chris got up to embrace.

"Thank you man. This really means a lot to me that you are acquiring my company. I wouldn't want to see it go to anyone else," Chris said.

"I've been wanting to get out here to LA and this was just the right deal at the right time."

Kyla was listening but not engaged. They had been talking all around her but she was completely tuning them out.

"Ain't that right?" Devin said.

"I'm sorry, you were talking to me?" Kyla asked.

"Yeah; I said, I'm lucky to have a great attorney like you that's always in my corner."

"Oh, yeah definitely," Kyla said dismissively.

"Is everything okay?"

"I'm okay. I need to make a phone call," Kyla said as she excused herself from the room.

She went into the hallway and called Alexis to see how things went with the pick-up. Alexis told her that she had given Melanie a dose of Tylenol to break her fever and that she was still asleep. She told her that the fever had gotten pretty high and if it didn't break, she was going to tell Vince to take her to the hospital. Being so far from her sick daughter caused her a pain that she was not used to, and one that she knew she could never get used to. All at once, her thoughts of long-term luxury and romance with Devin vanished. Tears began to silently fall from her eyes as she hung up. She didn't hear Devin come out into the hallway. He noticed her crying.

"I asked you earlier if everything was okay," Devin said.

"I didn't want to get into it during a business meeting but my daughter is sick and running a really high fever and I'm worried about her," Kyla responded.

"What can I do to make you feel better?"

"You want the honest answer?"

"Yes."

"I want you to fly me home."

"If that's what you want, I can get you there tonight."

"I'm really sorry. I know you probably had all of these plans for us and I really wanted to help you look for that house but my daughter has to come first."

"Listen, I understand. We have plenty of time to look at houses together, they aren't going anywhere. I want you to go and be with your daughter."

"You really are special. I think I just need some time to handle things on my end before I can jump into this with two feet. There are a lot of balls in the air right now with work, a pending divorce and my

162

daughter. You deserve to have someone that can be available for you and right not I just can't be."

"I've been a single man for a long time and I know what I want and need. I don't want you to worry about what's best for *me*; I want you to worry about what's best for *you*. If you decide that *I'm* what's best for *you* then we can move forward and if not, then I wish you well in whatever you decide. I'm not a selfish guy who wouldn't want you to take your time trying to figure things out. I'm not going to wait around forever but you know I dig you and I want to see where things can go. Nevertheless, I also understand your situation completely so go handle your business. There is no pressure or timeline here."

They wrapped up the conversations and headed out to the car. The driver took them back to the hotel, where Kyla checked out of her room and brought her things into Devin's room. They ordered room service for lunch and hung out for a bit before they headed back out to the airport. Devin made arrangements for her to go back home on a private jet. Once they reached the hanger, they got out of the car and he pulled her close. Silently, they stared into each other's eyes and kissed goodbye as he stroked her hair. Something inside of her told her that this was their last kiss. It was clear that things between them were over. He watched her board the plane and also felt the finality of the situation as she reached the top step of the plane. He blew her a kiss and the doors closed. She took a seat and waved to him out of the window.

Chapter 13

It's an early fall Sunday morning and Vince has been cleaning up his apartment and preparing to go to the gym and clear his head. He has a busy week ahead of him with work and a second session with the mediator planned for this Friday. Since Melanie's party a month ago any further talks between Kyla and him were at a standstill. He finished in the kitchen, shined the hardwood floors throughout the house, and decided to de-clutter the papers that he'd been accumulating. He picked up a stack of envelopes that had been piling up in the corner or his living room and decided to organize and purge what was no longer necessary to keep. As he was flipping through the envelopes he came across the letter that Kyla had written him a few months back. He tore the envelope open and sat down on the couch to read it.

As Vince read it carefully line by line, trying not to miss anything, tears silently rolled down his face. He began to imagine what would have happened had he just taken the time to listen to her months ago. Would they be in this predicament? Had he made a mess of things by not listening? He now understood that he hadn't caused her to stray before they were married. He saw that he had to decide whether to continue allowing his ego consume him or to forgive her. The letter made him question everything that he thought he knew about their relationship. He had reached a crossroads: should he swallow his pride and put his family back together or give up because it was too late? Looming over him was another question: if he moved forward with forgiveness, *would she forgive him for what he'd done with Liz*? He also considered whether or not she would be too bitter about how he'd treated her over the previous months.

Vince felt as though he owed it to himself to at least see if there was a chance to talk about what she wrote in her letter and see if there was still a chance for them. He had to get a game plan in place if he was going to have this difficult conversation with Kyla. Most importantly, he wanted her to know that he was ready to listen and possibly move forward.

The first thing he knew he had to do was to press the pause button on his relationship with Annette. She was getting in the way of his thought process. He knew he couldn't think rationally with her in the picture. He didn't want to break it off with her completely but he wanted to be sure that things with Kyla were absolutely over before they got too serious. In the short amount of time they were together, he did develop some feelings for Annette. She was a good woman, he thought, but getting his family back was more important. He picked up his phone and flipped through the pictures from Melanie's party and with every family photo he scrolled past, the more confident he became in his decision to fight for his relationship. He grabbed his keys and headed out the door to get to the gym.

Once Vince got to the gym he stretched and ran a few laps around the indoor track before heading for the weights. Just as he was about to start his weight lifting session his phone rang.

"Hello," Vince said, breathing heavily.

"Hey, I think we need to talk," Annette said.

"I can't right now, I'm at the gym."

"Okay, call me when you get done."

"Alright."

"What time do you think you'll be done?"

"I don't know, maybe an hour or so but I'll call you later," Vince said as he hung up the phone abruptly.

Vince went back to his workout and after about an hour he finished up and decided to drive over to his parents' house to talk to his dad for some advice. He pulled up in the driveway and used his key to get in. Once he got inside he hugged his mom and saw his dad sitting on the couch watching the Eagles pre-season game against the Steelers so he decided to join him.

"What's up, dad?" Vince asked.

"Nothing much, son, just watching this game." Mr. Preston responded.

"Who's winning?"

"It's tied up right now 10-10 but we got the ball in the red zone."

"I need some advice, dad."

"What's going on, son?"

165

"This thing with Kyla has me so confused right now."

"I tried to stay out of it. I know your mom got all involved but I wanted you to be able to make your own decision without having people tell you how to think or how to feel unless you asked for help. What is it that you're confused about?"

"I'm confused about whether or not I'm doing the right thing by divorcing her. Maybe we could have fought to save the marriage."

"Well it's not too late if you're having regrets, you aren't divorced yet."

"I know but I think mom was right in the beginning when she said that I needed to give people a chance to make mistakes."

"Vincent, we all make mistakes, nobody but GOD is infallible. Hell, I made mistakes in this marriage and luckily for me, your mother has a forgiving spirit."

"You cheated on mom?"

"I'm not saying *that* but I am saying that I've done some things that I'm not necessarily proud of. Your mother did a good job shielding it from you and your sisters. If she didn't forgive me, we wouldn't be where we are today."

"I know, but forgiveness is hard when you've been lied to."

"Haven't you lied to her before?"

"Yeah, but she doesn't know I lied."

"Then in that case, you are no better than her. If you hid the truth from her then you are being deceitful as well."

"I didn't look at it that way."

"We men never do. We want our women to be faithful, honest, and loyal but don't hold ourselves to the same standard."

"I try to be that way at least I thought I was with her."

"Then what is this business I heard about with you messing around with her best friend?"

"Dad that was a one-time thing. The girl came on to me after we had too many drinks and it got a little out of hand."

"Don't you think that should be punishment enough for her? In fact, I think that was worse than what *she* did."

"Kind of, but she had an emotional attachment to the dude that she was messing around with and that's the worst kind of affair."

"Have you talked to her about it or even tried to hear her side?"

"No, I just shut down. She left me a letter explaining everything but it took me months to read it and now I feel like I made a mistake and she could be gone forever."

"If you love her, then go get her son. Both of you did each other wrong and now you can make it right. Apologize to her and let her apologize to you face to face. Get your family back because you haven't been the same since you broke up."

"I knew you would keep it honest with me."

"I don't know why you didn't come to me before it got this far."

"I don't know either but I thought I could handle this by myself."

"That's why you have me, son. I'm always going to tell you the truth, even if it hurts."

"Thanks, dad," Vince said, as he reached over and gave his dad a manly embrace.

"Vincent, are you staying for dinner?" Mrs. Preston asked.

"You know it mom." Vince responded.

"Okay, I will fix you a plate when it's ready."

"Thanks."

Vince and his dad continued watching the game and around 6:30PM Mrs. Preston brought in a tray with two plates of food on it. The two men ate and yelled at the television as the game went on. After spending a few hours with his parents, Vince drove home to get ready for work, completely forgetting about Annette but she didn't forget about him. He came home, jumped in the shower and when he got out there was a text message from Annette reading, *"Did you forget about me?"* He responded, *"No, I'll call you in a few."* Annette decided not to wait for him and called him instead.

"I said I was going to call you in a few," Vince said, sounding annoyed when he answered the phone.

"That's what you said earlier but you never called and I told you I had something I really wanted to talk to you about," Annette said.

"Damn, I was having dinner with my parents."

"You didn't tell me that."

"Do I have to tell you everything?"

"No, but you said you would call me when you left the gym."

"I got sidetracked okay."

"There seems to be a lot of that lately."

"What are you talking about?"

"I'm talking about the fact that you have been distant and unavailable a lot lately. What's really going on?"

"I already told you, I've been dealing with a lot lately, especially with this divorce and my new promotion at work. All of this shit is stressful."

"You keep using this divorce as an excuse to pull away from me."

"It's not an excuse. I'm keeping it real with you; isn't that what you would want me to do or would you rather I lie?"

"I want you to talk to me and not pull away from me. It feels like you're trying to push me away."

"Why would I do that?"

"I think we really need to talk in person. I'm coming over there."

"No, I have my daughter."

"Really?"

"Yeah, so maybe tomorrow."

"Maybe?"

"I don't know if she's staying yet."

"Why don't you know that? I swear I feel like your ex has got you by the balls."

"By the balls? Bit... I'm done with this conversation because I might say some things that I can't take back so I'll holler," Vince said angrily, as he pressed the button to end the call.

Annette was beginning to feel him slipping away but she was determined to get him to hear her out. She really had more that she wanted to say but Vince was shutting her down. She tried calling him back a few times but he kept sending her to voicemail before turning off the phone. He waited about a half an hour before turning the phone on and saw several voicemails from Annette but he ignored them all and instead called Kyla. She let the phone ring a few times before answering it.

"Hello," she said, sounding half asleep.

"We need to talk?" Vince said.

"About what?"

"Us."

"There is no more us, so what are we talking about now."

"I'm coming over there."

"For what? What did I do now?"

"I'll talk to you about it when I get there."

"Okay."

Kyla sat up in the bed wondering what in the world he wanted to talk about because every conversation in the previous months had ended badly. The only thing she could think about was him wanting to discuss the mediation. But why tonight when the mediation wasn't for a few days? At any rate, she was getting herself ready for a fight because that's all they seem to do. After nearly half an hour, she heard the back door open up and she knew it was Vince. She heard him travel up the steps to her bedroom. He walked through the door and sat down on the bed next to her.

"What was so important that you had to come all the way over here?" Kyla asked.

"I read your letter," Vince responded very sincerely.

"Oh really. It only took you months but it's no longer important."

"So none of the things that you wrote apply anymore?"

"It all still applies but it's too late."

"Too late for what?"

"For us, we're too far gone."

"You know you don't mean that."

"Why don't I?" Kyla said angrily, as she got up out of the bed.

"Because I know you still love me and deep down inside you know I love you too," Vince said, as he stood up to approach her.

Tears began falling from Kyla's eyes as she said, "I've never stopped loving you but you hurt me. You treated me like your enemy for months. You ignored me, hung up on me and pushed me away."

Vince grabbed her by the hands and with tears filling his eyes said, "Baby you hurt me too. The thought of you being with another man tore me up inside. I couldn't stand the sight of you and I wanted you to hurt the way that I was hurting but baby I'm sorry. I just need to know one thing; do you still love him?

"No, I don't."

"Just tell me that you're done with him and I swear I will let it go."

Kyla looked away and then back at him and said, "I am done with him, I swear, but how do you expect me to forgive you for what you did to me with Liz. That shit cut like a knife. I could put up with you running around here with some strange woman that I don't know, but Liz, that was way below the belt."

"I don't know but what I did was wrong and I never should have been in that position to begin with. We were drunk and that's no excuse but I never slept with her."

"I still can't believe you are standing here now ready to repair this marriage when I've been asking for forgiveness for months."

"Kyla, I realize that I'm not perfect and I can't expect you to be either. It broke my heart to see you fall apart at that last mediation and I realized then that I still believed in us no matter how hard I tried to convince myself that I didn't."

"How do I know this is real and not just a temporary feeling?"

"I'm telling you that this is real and I'm willing to do whatever we need to do to fix us and get back to where we belong, if you're willing."

"I don't know," Kyla said, as she pulled away.

Vince pulled her back towards him, wrapped his arms around her waist, looked her straight in the eye and said, "I love you Kyla Marie Preston and I've never stopped. Please give us another chance."

With more tears running down her eyes Kyla responded, "I love you too and I do want to give us another chance."

Vince kissed her passionately and picked her up as she wrapped her legs around his waist and he spun her around to gently lay her onto the bed. He pulled up her shirt and started kissing her belly button and working his way up to her breast and then her lips again. He wasted no time snatching the night shirt off of her. She wasn't wearing any underwear and he knew that she slept bottomless. They continued kissing and as he removed his shorts and underwear simultaneous in one motion. She pulled his t-shirt over his head as he climbed on top of her inserting himself and they began making passionate love with all of the fireworks that would be expected from months of being away from one another. He pounded away like this could possibly be his last shot at ever being inside of her again. She gripped him so tightly around his back to feel him close to her that he could barely move. She wanted to feel every bit of him inside of her. They rolled around the bed changing positions like porn stars until they both reached their climax and their bodies became limp.

They rolled over into a spooning position as Vince held Kyla tight and said, "Damn I've missed you."

"I've missed you too," Kyla responded before they got up to clean up in the bathroom. Once they were done washing up and returned to the bedroom Vince kissed Kyla sweetly and asked, "Can I stay with you tonight?"

"I would love that," Kyla responded.

"We should stay home from work tomorrow. Do you have a sick day you could use?"

"I think I feel a fever coming on."

"Me too."

They laughed and got in the bed and fell off to sleep holding each other and hoping to never let go again.

Chapter 14

The next morning, Vince and Kyla woke up and cooked breakfast together. They were very playful, snapping each other with the dish towels in the kitchen. When breakfast was ready, they all ate together as a family for the first time in months. They decided to spend the day together making up for lost time so they called out of work and decided to stay in bed most of the day, talking and making love while entertaining Melanie in between. It had been a long time since they were able to do that and it felt good. Having finally gotten on the road to forgiveness, they knew that it would take time to return to where they once were, so they agreed to take things slowly. Kyla followed her therapist's advice by telling him the whole truth so that there were no more secrets between them to allow trust to be built again. Although they were eager to be a family again, they weren't planning to move back in together right away, but instead spend some nights together until they were ready to fully return to normalcy.

Throughout the day, Annette kept calling Vince's cell phone and it was beginning to feel as though she wasn't going to go away. Now that Kyla had agreed to work things out, he was going to have to let Annette go. He didn't want to hurt her feelings but, judging by the way she was calling his phone, he might have to cut her off cold turkey. When the evening came to an end, Vince collected his things to reluctantly head home to his apartment.

"Baby, I don't want to leave but I have to get home and get ready for work in the morning," Vince said.

"This is your home too, remember?" Kyla said.

"I know, but I meant my *temporary* home."

"I like the sound of temporary."

"I can't wait to get back here with you and Melanie full time but we'll work our way up to that. I can come stay here a few nights a week. We can use my apartment as our little hideaway in the city."

"Yes, after I burn some sage to get rid of the evil spirits that have been hiding in there that kept you away from me for so long."

"No sage needed because I'm all yours again."

"You better be," Kyla said, as she kissed Vince goodbye.

Vince headed out of the back door to his car and headed home. While in the car, he decided to call Annette back to break the news to her that it was over between them but he decided to wait until the morning because he'd had a great day with his family and didn't want to ruin it with an argument. He got home, got himself together and headed to bed. Just as he was falling asleep, he got a text message from Annette reading, *"Why are you avoiding me?"* He ignored the message and then turned his phone off.

The next morning when he got to work his assistant handed him his messages as he walked to his office and there were several from Annette. He threw them in the trash without reading a single one. He went on to begin his busy work day that consisted of attending a team meeting, going over portfolios and talking to clients. Shortly after 10:00AM, he got a call from his assistant.

"Mr. Preston, there is a Ms. Jennings down in the lobby to see you but I didn't see her on your schedule. Do you have time to see her or shall I tell her to make an appointment?"

"Tell her to stay right there, I'll go down there in a second."

"Okay, sir."

"Thank you."

Vince took a deep breath and collected his thoughts before going down to the lobby. This was beginning to get out of hand. He was wondering why she just couldn't take a hint when he stopped answering her phone calls. Now she was showing up at his job and this wasn't a good sign. The last time a woman showed up at his job, it wasn't to bring good news either. He was happy his job had such tight security. Once he got off of the elevator, he approached the security desk and went on the side where Annette was standing. She didn't look like her usual self, instead she looked frazzled and upset.

"Why are you showing up at my job like this?" Vince asked in a forceful tone.

"Because you won't take any of my calls and I need to talk to you."

"I can't talk right now; I'm in the middle of a meeting."

"What about lunch?"

"Okay, I can do that. I will meet you at the 21 at noon."

"Alright, I'll see you then."

"Cool. Do me a favor?"

"What's that?"

"Don't ever come to my job unannounced again."

"I can't make any promises."

"I'm serious," Vince said, as he walked away.

Vince headed back to his office to continue working until noon. He alerted his assistant that he had to run out for lunch and to hold all of his calls until he returned. He hurried over to the 21 restaurant a few blocks down to meet Annette. He was hoping to hear her out and let her down gently. He waited for her in the lobby and they walked in and grabbed a table.

"What is so urgent that you would show up at my job?" Vince asked, as they sat down.

"I didn't like the way that we ended the conversation the other day," Annette said.

"So you call me a million more times and show up at my job to tell me that?"

"No, I wanted to tell you that I'm falling in love with you and this thing with your wife has me on edge because I don't like how you've been acting lately since the divorce mediation has started."

Vince sighed because he knew he had to tell her at this point before her feelings got any deeper so he said, "I've been having second thoughts about the divorce."

"Second thoughts?"

"Yes, I don't think I can go through with it."

"You still love her?"

"Yes, I do and I want to work things out with her. I'm sorry but I'm going to have to stop seeing you."

Annette started to cry and then yelled, "I'm sorry too because I'm pregnant!"

"Pregnant? Don't play with me. Are you saying this to get back at me for breaking up with you?"

"I'm not playing? Why would I make that up?"

"I don't know what you might say these days to get what you want. So you're saying I'm the father?"

"Yes, it's YOUR baby!"

"Are you sure? We used protection."

"Not every time."

"How far along are you?"

"Eight weeks."

"I need proof."

Annette reached into her purse and pulled out a sonogram, slapped it on the table and said, "Is that proof enough for you?"

Vince examined the sonogram carefully and saw that it was real and asked, "What are you going to do?"

"What do you mean what am *I* going to do? I'm keeping *our* baby."

"I'm going to need a DNA test."

"That's so typical of you men. You don't want to own up to your responsibility. We had sex and you got me pregnant, so deal with it. It looks like you will be super dad times two."

Vince sat there stunned and put his hands on his head in disbelief. He started feeling like the walls were caving in on him and like the air was being sucked out of the room. All he could ask himself is, *"How could I let this happen? Why now?"*

Vince stood up without placing an order and threw money on the table to pay whatever bill she might incur and said, "Look, I gotta get back to work. I can't deal with this right now."

"So you're just going to leave me here and walk away after I told you I'm having your baby?"

"I'm sorry but I need time to process all of this," Vince said, as he walked out of the door.

Annette sat in the booth crying uncontrollably as the server came over to check on her.

"Are you okay?" the server asked.

"I'm fine, I just had a fight with my boyfriend."

"Can I get you anything?"

"Water would be great for now."

Annette sat there and collected her thoughts and drank the water that the server brought to the table. She tipped her for the water, put the rest of the money in her purse and left. Meanwhile, Vince was walking back to work with his new found happiness beginning to crumble. He was trying to figure out how he was going to break the news to Kyla and if this would be a game changer for them getting back together. He thought maybe he could convince Annette not to have the baby but that would be shameful considering how much he believed in a woman's right to choose. But desperate times called for desperate measures.

He got back to the office and just couldn't concentrate so he decided to call out sick like he had the day before. He needed to collect his thoughts and figure out what he was going to do and how long he could keep this a secret. He had enough money to pay her to go away but Kyla might catch on to money mysteriously leaving the house. He thought about setting up a private trust for the baby but then the thought of a kid in the world without a dad didn't sit well with him either. He just needed to buy time and figure out his next move while he and Kyla worked on getting things back on track.

Kyla called Vince at work and his assistant informed her that he had gone home sick. She was worried so she called to check on him and he told her that he had a migraine headache so he went home to lie down. After Kyla left work, she decided to surprise Vince with dinner at his apartment after she picked up Melanie. She parked the car and called Vince to get his help with the bags and Melanie. Once he got to the car he leaned in to give her a kiss as she was getting out. When she was fully out of the car, she happened to look over Vince's shoulder to catch a surprising glimpse of Liz walking pass them. Liz slowed down and the two of them locked eyes as Kyla pulled Vince in for another embrace just to show Liz that she was wrong about him not forgiving her. Liz picked up her pace once she realized what she had just witnessed. Kyla felt a small victory inside because she could see the look of disgust on Liz's face. Once they were inside the apartment, she began getting the food ready for everyone and she noticed that Vince was rather quiet and withdrawn.

"Is everything okay, babe?" Kyla questioned.

"I'm okay, I just have a lot on my mind and my head still hurts a little. I've had a very stressful day at work."

"You wanna talk about it?"

"No, I just want to enjoy my family," Vince said as he walked over to the kitchen to kiss Kyla on the cheek before returning to Melanie in the living room.

They spent a few more hours together before Kyla and Melanie departed for their home, which helped to ease a little bit of his tension but deep down inside, he knew their happiness would only be temporary. He wanted to hold on to as long as he could.

* * *

Sal was heading home after picking up Aaron from the daycare, which he rarely did. Just as they were settling down to eat, he heard a knock at the door. He got up to see who it was before opening the door since he knew he wasn't expecting anybody. When the door swung open, Aaron put his chicken nugget down and yelled, "Auntie", as he ran to jump into her arms.

"Hi, Aaron. Auntie missed you," Annette said.

"I missed you too," Aaron said, as he gave her a kiss.

"What's up sis?" Sal said, as he reached over to give her a hug.

"Hey, big bro," she responded.

"What brings you over here? I mean you've been back for months and we hardly ever see you. Shit, you live right up the street."

"I know, I know. I'm bad at visiting. You know me, always the loner but I need to talk," she said, as she joined them at the table.

"What's going on?" Sal asked in a concerned tone.

Tears started to fill up in her eyes as she said, "I'm in trouble."

"What kind of trouble?"

"The worse kind."

"Jail type trouble?"

"No, worse."

"Well I don't' know what could be worse than jail."

"Being pregnant by a married man could be worse than jail."

"Wow, that's pretty fucked up. How did you do that? Never mind, that's a dumb ass question. What are you doing messing around with a married man anyway? You know that's playing with fire. Take it from me, *I* know."

"He was getting a divorce when we met and now he's backing out of it."

"So he's getting back with his wife now after you told him you were pregnant?"

"I told him I was pregnant after he told me that he was getting back with her."

"He probably thinks you're lying."

"Yeah he does but I showed him the sonogram."

"Are you keeping it?"

"Yeah but of course he wants a DNA test before he gets involved."

"He better step up and do the right thing or I'm going to be on his ass."

"I'm not sure that he will but we'll see."

"Why do you want to keep the baby?"

"You know I always wanted a family. That's why me and Johnnie broke up because he didn't want children."

"You're not getting a family though; you're getting a baby. Those are two different things."

"The baby will be my family."

"Yes, but you will be raising this baby alone and trust me, it's hard work without a support system. I mean, I have mom to pick him up from daycare every day and keep him until I get home but other than that Aaron is basically all my responsibility. There are times that I really resent Alicia for leaving Aaron because I didn't want to be with her. He needs two parents to be involved and so will your baby."

"I understand that but this will be different. Alicia is in Vegas and this baby's father is right here in Philly. I think he'll come around eventually. Perhaps this is just a phase that he's going through because we've been arguing lately."

"You honestly think that getting back with his wife is just a phase?"

"I do because he wasn't' thinking about her until I started nagging him about her. He basically hated her but I think I pushed him back into her arms."

"Why were you so concerned about her?"

"Because I was curious. He never mentioned her name, he wouldn't tell me anything about her. I just found out that she was an attorney."

"Where did you meet this guy?"

"At Aaron's daycare."

"What's his name?"

"I'd rather not say. I don't want you running around trying to strong arm him like dad would do. I want time to process all of this and work things out. You'll meet him in due time. I'll let you know if I need you to get involved though."

"Okay, I'll spare his life for now."

"Lucky him. So who's the lucky lady in *your* life?"

"I don't have just one. You know me; I'm forever the ladies' man. Seriously though, I still kick it with Kyla every now and again. She's about the only one that I ever took seriously."

"I can't believe that you're still seeing that girl after all of these years. I don't know why you never married her. I always liked her for you."

"I always liked her too and would have married her but she married some other clown."

"I guess I've been out of the loop since I moved to New York or I would've known that. I should've come around more but I promise to do better. I really do miss my family and, now that I'm expecting, I need to be around family more anyway.

"You have been gone too long. I never thought you would come back."

"I couldn't stay there any longer since I broke up with Johnnie and I came right home and got myself into some more shit. Big bro. I've held you long enough and I need to get out of here to clear my head. I have a lot on my mind."

"Okay and stop being a stranger. Come see us sometimes and we will do the same. Maybe now that you're pregnant, I can add you to my babysitting list so that you can get some practice before your little one comes."

"Ha, you wish. I'm going to enjoy my next several months of freedom."

Annette got up and she and Sal hugged tightly before she headed out the door to her house. When she got home, she found Vince sitting on the swing on her porch.

"What are you doing here?" Annette asked.

"We need to talk," Vince said.

"Why do we need to talk now all of a sudden? Did you go home and tell your precious wife about our baby and she put you out?"

"No I didn't. I don't know when I'm going to tell her but I need some time to sort all of this out."

"Time? In less than eight months, you will be a dad again. How long do you expect me to wait for you to figure your life out?"

"I don't know but are you sure you want to keep the baby?"

"I already told you that I am keeping it."

"I'm sure that there's nothing that I can do to change your mind but I want you to understand that things will be complicated."

"I know they will be but we will manage."

"If the baby is mine, I will take full responsibility both financially and physically."

"There is no question that this is your baby so you can stop saying 'if' and I'd like you to be involved throughout the pregnancy."

"I don't know how involved I can be at this time."

"You can come to appointments with me."

"I might be able to do that depending on when they are and if I'm available."

"You'll have to make yourself available."

"It's not that simple and you know it."

"You're the one making this complicated. We can still be together."

"No we can't. I was serious when I said I was getting back with my wife."

"We'll see how serious she is about getting back with you once she finds out that there will be a new baby in your life."

"This isn't a competition."

"I'm not trying to compete but things between us were going great until I pushed you away."

"You didn't push me away. I never stopped loving *her*, I was just fooling myself. And this thing between us was temporary. You came into my life at a very low point and I fell for you but it wasn't real."

"What do you mean it wasn't real?"

"It was a fantasy. You were taking my mind off of my reality."

"This baby isn't a fantasy and I am a real person with real feelings."

"I never meant to hurt you but I never meant for it to go this far between us either."

"You were using me?"

"Not exactly. I enjoyed spending time with you but I wasn't ready to fully commit to another relationship."

"Why didn't you tell me that in the beginning?"

"Because it never came up and I was just going with the flow."

"Going with the flow got us here and now you have to deal with it."

"I will deal with it but I would appreciate some space while I'm trying to deal."

"Space?"

"Yes, space. That means you have to stop calling me, texting me and showing up at my job unless it's a real emergency."

"How long is this gag order in effect?"

"Just until I'm able to get everyone on board with this situation."

"I'll give you two months and that's it. After that, all bets are off."

"Okay, I can appreciate that."

Annette opened up her door and headed inside. Once she shut the door, she watched Vince disappear down the steps and out of sight. The sight of him leaving made her feel like he would never come back. She leaned up against the door and cried tears of sadness that could fill buckets.

* * *

Kyla and Vince had successfully rekindled their love affair. They were going on dates, spending plenty of time together at their homes and even got their families back on the same page. He started moving some of his clothing back into their suburban home to make the transition fuller. They seemed to have pressed the gas pedal on their reconciliation, even though they had agreed to take it slow. Vince didn't know how much time he had left with his newfound happiness with this huge baby secret looming over him so he wanted to savor every moment as long as he could. He was being unusually nice by showering Kyla with lavish gifts and even taking her on expensive weekend getaways. His two-month window was coming to a close and he still couldn't find a way to come clean about the baby. Deep down inside he was hoping that it was all just a dream or that she really wasn't pregnant. She didn't try to contact him so he thought that maybe she went away but right on cue at the two-month mark, she called.

"Hello," Vince said, as he answered the phone tentatively.

"I have an appointment tomorrow at 8th and Market and you need to be there," Annette said.

"What time?"

"2:30."

"I have a meeting at that time."

"Find a way to make it work."

"I'll see what I can do."

"That's not good enough. If you don't show up, I'm going to the daycare and waiting for your wife to pick up Melanie and I'm going to tell her everything."

"Now you're playing with fire."

"You've already done that so it's my turn."

"Are you threatening me?"

"Not a threat but I'm tired of waiting," Annette said, before hanging up.

Now Vince had to try to think two steps ahead of her because she was starting to get all *Fatal Attraction* on him. He didn't like being threatened and he wasn't going to jump because she said jump. When he got home that night he told Kyla that he would be picking Melanie up from daycare for the rest of the week to avoid any confusion. He worked his schedule out with his assistant to make sure he didn't have any late meetings that would prevent him for picking her up. When Vince didn't show for the appointment, Annette got really angry and called his phone repeatedly until he blocked her number. The next day when he showed up for work, Annette was waiting for him in the lobby of his building again. He didn't want to make a scene because people at his job would know his secret and he couldn't risk anyone finding out and perhaps leaking the information to Kyla. He quietly pulled her outside of the building to talk. By this point she was beginning to look pregnant so now it was real.

"Look, I already told you to stop showing up at my job," Vince said, through clinched teeth.

"You missed our appointment yesterday." Annette said angrily.

"I told you that I had a meeting and I couldn't make it."

"Time's up, Vince. I'm going to your wife."

"How exactly are you going to do that?"

"I told you already."

"Leave her out of this!"

"Too late."

"What do you want?"

"I told you already. I want you to get on board with this baby."

"Why are you making this so difficult?"

"Because men like you always get away with doing women however you want. You think you can win us over with your charm and good looks, wine and dine us, fuck us until we can't think straight and then

182

leave us for the next one or in this case the old one. Not this time. You're going to own up to your shit."

"Annette, this baby has you acting crazy."

"You haven't seen crazy yet."

"I'm done here; I have to get to work."

"Come to my house tonight at 7:00PM. Don't be late either."

"If I come over there, will you stop with all of this nonsense?"

"That depends."

"On?"

"You'll see."

Vince went to work and all he kept thinking about was how out of hand this situation has gotten. Once he was done for the day, he went to pick up Melanie and drop her off to his mother. He called Kyla to tell her that he had a last-minute client meeting so Melanie was with his mother and she could pick her up from there and that he'd be home for dinner around 8:30. He raced over to Annette's house so that he could see what she wanted and to set her straight once and for all for her threatening behavior. He rang the doorbell and when the door opened up Sal and Vince locked eyes.

"Is Annette here?" Vince said, thinking that the man's face looks familiar.

"What the fuck are you doing here?" Sal asked angrily.

"I should be asking you the same question?"

"Annette is my sister. Please tell me that you are NOT the married motherfucker that got her pregnant!"

"And if I am?"

"Then you need your ass whipped," Sal said, as he sucker punched Vince without warning.

Vince swung back on Sal realizing who he actually was and the two started fighting going blow for blow knocking over furniture in the living room. They weren't just fighting over Annette; they were fighting over Kyla too. Annette ran in and tried to break it up and got knocked to the ground.

"Stop!" she yelled at them.

"I told you to take care of Kyla, didn't I? And this is what you do to her?" Sal yelled between punches.

"I'm taking care of her real good. This is for fucking my wife." Vince said as he punched Sal in the face again.

"I knew your ass was a snake when I met you. You don't deserve Kyla or my sister," Sal countered with a body shot.

"Kyla?" Annette yells as she tried to break them apart again.

Breathing heavily and wiping blood from his lip, Sal responds, "Yeah, he's married to Kyla."

"Your old girlfriend Kyla?" Annette asks.

"Yeah," Sal responded.

Annette fell back on the couch and balled up into a fetal position crying uncontrollably at this point. Her emotions were all over the place. She was angry, embarrassed, and sick all at the same time.

"Sal, you need to call Kyla NOW!" Annette yelled through her tears.

"No, let me handle it," Vince said.

"Tell her that I'm sorry," Annette said, as she cried even harder, while continuing to rock back and forth.

"What are you sorry for? You didn't get yourself pregnant. He's the one that should be sorry," Sal said, pointing to Vince.

"None of us would be in this position if *you* hadn't slept with Kyla in the first place," Vince said, talking to Sal.

"Man, please. She was mines first and she's gonna always be mine. You think your little ring is stopping anything. I can have her whenever I get ready," Sal said.

Vince stood up to swing on Sal again but Annette jumped in the way and yelled, "ENOUGH! You two have to stop fighting and we all need to figure this out. Vince I called you over here to tell you that we are having a boy."

"Wow," Vince said.

"Wow? Is that all you have to say?" Sal said through clinched teeth.

"I don't know what else to say," Vince said.

"Say you're going to take care of your son, that's what the fuck you need to say," Sal said.

"I already told her that I would take care of my responsibilities so that's not an issue," Vince said.

"Now you need to go home to your wife and tell her what is really going on. This is one crazy ass story and I bet she leave yo ass," Sal said.

"I forgave her for fucking with you so now it's her turn," Vince said.

"Yeah but I didn't get her pregnant either so good luck with that," Sal said.

"You know what man, FUCK YOU! Fuck you for thinking that you could have my wife and break up our family. Fuck you for thinking that she still wants your sorry ass and fuck you for even existing," Vince said as he headed out the door.

Once he got in his car, he knew that he was in for a long night because there was no way he was going to get away without Kyla seeing him all bruised and bloodied. He prepared his speech all the way home, rehearsing it over and over. Nothing that he said made any sense because there was no easy way to say he had a baby by Sal's sister. This one was surely the hardest test of his life and he prayed he could pass it. The odds were not in his favor.

Chapter 15

Kyla was at home preparing a romantic candlelight dinner for her and Vince. Melanie had already eaten at her grandmother's house so Kyla gave her a bath and put her to bed. She wanted to thank him for stepping up this week with Melanie and to share some good news with him. After taking the food out of the oven and setting the table, she lit the candles and waited for him to walk through the door. It was getting late and she started to worry. She called him to check on him.

"Hello," Vince said.

"Is everything okay?" Kyla asked, curiously.

"Yeah. I'll be home in fifteen minutes."

"Okay, I'll see you soon," she said, before hanging up.

Once she hung up, she waited a few minutes before re-lighting the candles that she had blown out because they were burning low. The food was still warm so all she had to do was fix their plates when he got in. She sat down on the couch as she continued to wait. She saw Vince pull into the garage but noticed that he didn't immediately get out of the car. His heart was racing a thousand beats per minute and he was so nervous, he felt like he would vomit. He sat there praying that Kyla was in a forgiving mood. He prayed that he wouldn't lose his family again but he was only a few minutes from finding out his fate. Finally, he got out of the car and slowly approached the house. Before he could get his key in the door, it swung open and he saw Kyla's beautiful face staring at him under a candlelit glow and his heart sunk.

"Welcome home, baby," Kyla said.

He looked at her with sad eyes and quietly said, "Thank you."

"What's wrong? Baby are *you* okay?"

"Come sit down. We need to talk."

"Vince you're scaring me. What's going on?"

Vince took Kyla by the hand and led her to the couch, turned to face her and said, "You know I love you right?"

"Yes, I do but what is all of this about?"

"I'm getting to that, just let me finish."

"Okay."

"I am so happy to finally have you back in my life and I want to be the husband that you deserve to have. I don't ever want us to be apart again. I want us to always be a family."

"Me too baby, but why do you look so sad."

"Kyla, I know that I didn't handle the situation in the best way when I found out about Sal and I'm sorry. I also did some things that I'm not necessarily proud of either but I hope that you can find it in your heart to forgive me as well."

"Vince, we've been over that already and we've forgiven each other. What did you do that I don't know about already? I mean what could be worse than what you did with Liz?"

He put his head down and said, "Remember the woman you saw me with at that restaurant a while back?"

"Yeah."

"Well ummm."

"Spit it out."

Vince took a deep breath and said, "She's pregnant and she says I'm the father."

Kyla yelled out, "WHAT! NO! How could this be happening?"

"I didn't intend for this to happen."

Kyla bust into uncontrollable tears, ran upstairs to their bedroom, and slammed the door. She slid down the wall onto the floor sobbing in the dark. She couldn't believe it. She wondered how this could happen when they had just gotten back together. They were supposed to be happy and getting a fresh start. So many thoughts were going through her head as she tried to process what he had just told her but she just couldn't wrap her head around any of it. This felt like a punch in the face by karma and she was trying to deal with the blow. Vince gave her some time to deal with things before trying to continue the conversation. After about ten minutes, he slowly crept upstairs and knocked on the door.

"Kyla, talk to me," Vince pleaded.

Kyla got up and slowly opened the door before going back to her position on the floor. He walked toward her, got down on the floor beside her, wrapped his arms around her and they hugged until she was decidedly ready to talk.

"Do you love her?" Kyla asked, through the tears.

"No, I don't," Vince said, very sincerely.

"Is she keeping the baby?"

"Yes, she is too far along not to."

"How far along is she?"

"Four and a half months."

"I can't believe this. Why can't we be happy? Maybe it's not meant for us and this is GOD's way of saying that we don't belong together."

"Don't say that. I'm sorry and I know you're hurt right now but we do belong together."

"If that is the case, why is everything trying to tear us apart?"

"It's all a test of our strength and faith and we can get through this if you're willing to try."

"This is too much for me right now. I don't know if I can handle a baby that's not mines."

"I need you right now. Please don't say that. Don't walk away from what we're building."

"This just changes so many things between us."

"Nothing has to change. I didn't mean for any of this to happen. I used protection with her so I don't even know if it's really my baby.

"You didn't use protection because she's pregnant and you think it's yours or you wouldn't be telling me this."

"I told her that I need a DNA test."

"You made me do the same thing and Melanie was yours. You wanna know the worst part about all of this?"

"What's that?"

"I was preparing a romantic dinner to surprise you with the very same news."

"You're pregnant," he said, with excitement in his voice.

"Yes. I am," Kyla said, with the sound of disappointment.

Vince's eyes got big and he asked, "When did you find this out?"

"I had been feeling sick and lightheaded lately so I made an appointment to check things out and the doctor came back and told me that I was pregnant. He did an ultrasound and found out that I am six weeks along."

He grabbed her belly and said, "That's good news, I'm going to be a dad again."

She pushed his hands away and asked, "Is that how you acted when she told you that she was pregnant too?"

"No, I was disappointed. I don't want to have a baby with her but I guess I don't get a say in that."

"Neither do I. I'm not going to lie; I don't want to deal with an outside child competing for your attention. Every time I look at that child, it will be a constant reminder of how it got here."

"I understand where you're coming from but I'm his father so we're going to have to find a way to include him. He didn't ask to be here, nor can he help the circumstances under which he was brought here."

"Him?"

"Yeah, she's having a boy."

"So this random chick is going to be the first to give you a legacy. GREAT! Now I'm really done," Kyla said, as she threw her hands in the air.

"She might be having my first son but she won't have *me* though. I'll be right here with you and our family."

"I don't know about that," Kyla said, as she got up to turn on the lights.

Vince was so happy to hear that Kyla was pregnant again that he failed to mention the most important aspect of this story but he didn't want to ruin the happiness right now. He got up to follow Kyla as she walked toward the bathroom. He pulled her into an embrace and tried to kiss her but she refused.

"What happened to your face," She asked curiously.

Forgetting all about the bruises he responded, "I got into a fight."

"A fight! With who?"

Vince took a deep and said the one name he hated most, "Sal."

"Sal! Why the hell were you fighting Sal?"

"The woman we have been talking about all of this time is named Annette and apparently that is his sister. When I went to her house to talk about the baby, he answered the door and punched me in the face so we fought."

Kyla immediately became sick to her stomach, ran to the bathroom and started throwing up. She collapsed onto the bathroom floor in horror.

She laid there screaming, "Oh my GOD" repeatedly. She was so overcome with emotion that she nearly fainted. He ran into the bathroom and put her head into his lap and stroked her hair as she cried. Tears began to run down his face onto her arms because he knew that this might be the end for them. She wouldn't even look at him.

After what felt like a lifetime of them lying on the bathroom floor she finally yelled out, "Take me to her. NOW!"

"How am I supposed to do that with Melanie here?"

"FIGURE IT OUT!"

"Let's be rational about this. It's late and I don't think it would be a good idea. Let's just calm down and sleep on it. We can go tomorrow."

"Don't tell me how to think! I want to go to her house now! As a matter of fact, move out of my way," Kyla screamed, as she pushed him aside.

Vince was so confused because Kyla got up off of the floor and started behaving erratically. She was throwing things around the room and having what appeared to be a tantrum. He watched her for about five minutes before restraining her by the arms to keep her from doing something that might cause her to suffer a miscarriage. She broke away from him and ran downstairs to grab her cell phone and call her sister. Alexis answered after a few rings.

"Hey, sis," Alexis said.

"I need you to come over here." Kyla said, with panic in her voice.

"What's wrong?"

"It's an emergency and we need someone to watch Melanie."

"Is everyone okay?"

"Not exactly."

"I'm on my way," Alexis said, as she hung up in a hurry.

Kyla stayed downstairs pacing back and forth and talking to herself. Vince tried to plead with her to calm down to no avail. After about twenty minutes, the doorbell rang and it was Alexis. Kyla opened the door and saw her sister who noticed how upset she was.

"What happened?" Alexis asked, as she looked at Vince for answers.

"We need to go but I will fill you in when we get back," Kyla said, as she grabbed Vince by the hand and led him to the back door to get to his car.

* * *

It was nearly 10:30PM as Vince and Kyla took the quiet ride to
Chestnut Hill from their suburban home in Delaware County. Kyla stared
out of the window throughout the entire ride and refused to even look at
Vince. She was so disgusted with him, with herself and by what was to
come. She had no real direction for how this conversation would go but she
knew that there wouldn't be any violent behavior because they were both
pregnant. She grew up having a fondness for Annette when she was a
young child. She thought of her as a little sister but lost touch with her
when she moved to New York as a pre-teen to go to a boarding school.
Annette never really came back to Philly and it was no wonder that Kyla
didn't recognize her at the restaurant. They pulled up to her street and
parked the car. They had to walk half way down the block to get to her
house. Once they got on the porch Kyla knocked on the door. When
Annette didn't immediately answer, Kyla banged harder.

"Calm down," Vince said.

"Don't tell me to come down," Kyla snipped.

"We don't want to wake the neighbors."

"Do you think I give a fuck about the neighbors?"

"That's obvious. Maybe she's asleep."

"Well she needs to wake her ass up."

After a few more hard knocks, Kyla started kicking the door with
the back of her shoe and Vince pulled her to the side and said, "Okay, now
you're going overboard."

"She better come to this door, that's all I know."

"What are you going to do if she doesn't? Break it down? Come on
Kyla, you are taking this too far."

A few seconds later, lights started turning on in the living room as
Annette pulled back the curtain to see both Vince and Kyla standing in
front of the door. She was stunned. They could hear her unlocking all of
the locks before cracking open the door. Kyla took one look at her and
could see why Vince was attracted to her because even without make up or
her hair done, she was gorgeous just like her brother and all Kyla could say
to herself was, *"Damn you Roccos for being so beautiful"*.

"What are you doing here?" Annette asked curiously.

"You know why we're here, don't act surprised" Kyla responded.

"I'm not surprised, just confused," Annette said.

"Confused about what?"

"Why you would drive all the way over here so late."

"I wanted to see you face to face. Are you gonna let us in or do you want your neighbors to know about this love square that we all have going on here?"

"Come on in," Annette said, as she opened the door to let them in.

Vince wasn't saying anything because he couldn't believe that his life had come to this and that he was currently sitting in the middle of two women who were both carrying his children. Kyla did all of the talking and led most of the conversation just like an attorney. Vince noticed that Annette didn't seem like the same tough girl who was showing up at his job and threatening him. Annette showed them to the living room couch where they all sat down.

"First of all, Kyla, I want you to know that I truly am sorry," Annette said, very humbly.

"What are you sorry for?" Kyla asked.

"Dating your husband. I honestly didn't know that *you* were his wife at the time. He never told me anything about you, not even your name."

Kyla turned to Vince and said, "Why didn't you tell her about me?"

"Because I didn't think she needed to know anything about you. The divorce was between us so there was no need to talk about you to her," Vince responded.

"But you *did* know that he was still married so why would you date *anybody's* husband, even if he wasn't' mine?" Kyla asked Annette.

"I did know that he was married but he told me that you were going through a divorce," Annette responded.

"Men like to use vague language because we weren't going through anything. Did he tell you that I never signed the papers when he served me? So basically the whole time that he was seeing you, the divorce hadn't even gotten started."

"No, he didn't tell me that. All he told me was that he was divorcing you because you were cheating on him and judging from the fight he and my brother had earlier, I'm guessing it was with him?"

"Yes and I can't say that I'm proud of what I did but the situation with your brother happened before Vince and I were even married."

"Sal told me the whole story today. You really broke his heart; you know that right?"

"I'm not here to discuss your brother and his feelings or to chastise you for sleeping with my husband because it's a done deal and now you're pregnant. I *am* here to see what it is that you want from him or from us, because it's obvious that you are keeping the baby?"

"I just want him to be a father to our son."

"He's going to do that, whether we're together or not because that is the type of man that he is but you do understand that he doesn't want to be with you?"

"He's made that clear. He has repeatedly told me that he wants to be with you."

"Umm hum," Kyla said, as she gave Vince the serious side eye.

"I wish that none of this happened but we can't take it back. Now all we can do is find a way to make this work for everyone."

"I think you're living in some sort of fantasy world if you think that we can all just be one happy family. You're on some you, me, and baby makes three type of shit. No offense but your baby is in the way."

"In the way of what? Your perfect little family? Why does this have to be all about you? You need to get over yourself because he will be a part of your lives, whether you like it or not."

"Well your son's father is going to have his hands full because we're also expecting again so good luck finding time to fit *your* kid in."

"Hold up, hold up. The both of you are sitting here talking about me like I'm not even in the room or like I can't decide what is best for my own children," Vince interrupted angrily, as he snapped out of his out-of-body experience.

"Do you really know what you've gotten yourself into?" Kyla snapped.

"Actually I do. I fully understand what has happened and how it happened. I'm a grown man who is capable of taking care of my responsibilities. These are my children and I plan to do right by ALL of them and that means spending time *with* them and money *on* them. And I do mean ALL of them. Unfortunately, Kyla, Annette is right, we will all have to work together for this situation to work and be amicable," Vince said.

"I just don't know if I can do that. And just to be clear, Sal is now your baby's uncle. He will be in our lives forever so I hope that you are ready for *that*," Kyla said.

Vince hadn't thought of that but this was his new reality whether he liked it or not. The man at the center of all of this confusion, who was probably asleep right now comfortably in his bed, will now be indirectly related to him and the thought of that made him a little sick inside.

Vince turned to both of the ladies and said, "You two can debate this all night, but the reality is, we have a long road ahead of us and children are coming. Kyla we need to get home to Melanie and you both need some time to collect your thoughts. I want you both to have healthy babies and this stress can't be good for either of you. I apologize for putting your both in this situation and I'm ready to move forward. Let's go!" Vince demanded, as he grabbed Kyla's arm to pull her to the door.

Kyla reluctantly stood up and said, "I don't apologize to either one of you for how I feel but I do need to get home to my daughter. Annette, I don't know if we'll ever get to a point where we are cool again but I'm just asking you to respect my marriage from this point on."

"What does that mean?"

"It means that you don't get priority on anything because *I'm* his wife and you will have to take a back seat because his family comes first."

"My son will be his family too."

"Vince, you need to talk some sense into her because I'm done," Kyla said, as they left the house.

They got back into the car to take the ride back home. Vince just wanted this nightmare to be over. He prayed for better days ahead but somehow he knew that things would be complicated from here on out. It was well after midnight when they pulled into their driveway.

Kyla turned to Vince and said, "You can drop me off and go."

"What do you mean?" Vince asked.

"I mean just what I said. I don't want to see your face right now or maybe ever."

"So you're putting me out?"

"You're not all the way back in yet. It's not like you don't have a place to go. You made sure of that."

"What was all of that you said back there at Annette's house about us being a family and me being your husband."

"I was stating current facts. You *are* my husband and we *are* a family but that doesn't mean it will stay that way."

"I don't get you. You ask for forgiveness, I give it to you but when the shoe is on the other foot, you are acting the very same way that I acted."

"You don't like it do you?"

"No, I don't."

"It's not fair, is it? It doesn't feel good to have your indiscretions held over your head and the fate of your family in question? Now you know how I feel."

"And so do you."

"But I didn't come away with a baby."

"Not for the lack of trying. Let's just say you got lucky."

Kyla just sat there for a minute and ingested that bit of truth that he just served her. In her effort to make him feel the way that she felt when he left her for cheating, she had not realized that this had all come full circle. The guilt, the lies, the emotions and the shame of breaking up their marriage. This time, though, everyone will know that their fairytale had a crack in it because they wouldn't be able to hide a baby.

"I'm going to make sure that you get in the house safely and I will go to the apartment. I'll give you some space but I'm not letting you go again. I promise, I will fight for us," Vince said.

Kyla was so mentally and physically exhausted that she just went in the house and closed the door without saying another word. When she got inside, Alexis was asleep on the couch and jumped up when she heard the back door slam.

"Is everything okay? Where is Vince?" Alexis asked.

"I don't want to talk about it," Kyla said.

"Do you want me to stay?"

"Yeah, I do. I just want you to give me a hug and tell me that everything will be okay like you used to do when we were kids."

Alexis walked over to her sister, gave her a big hug and Kyla cried on her shoulder. She rubbed her back and said, "Everything is going to be okay. Whatever you're going through right now GOD will work it out."

The two went upstairs and Alexis called Chris to let her know that she would be staying with Kyla for the night. Kyla put her pajamas on and curled up next to her sister like she used to do as a child and they both fell asleep.

* * *

The next morning, Kyla woke up and took Melanie to daycare. She called out of work and drove over to the restaurant to see her mother, who was preparing for her lunch opening. Mrs. Carter knew something had to be up because he daughter usually doesn't pop over during work hours unless something was wrong. She could tell that Kyla wasn't going to work because she was wearing sweatpants and no makeup.

"Hey, baby girl," Mrs. Carter said, as they hugged.

"Hey, mom," Kyla said.

"You off today?"

"I took the day off. I needed a mental health day and I thought I would stop by and see you."

"What's wrong?"

"Why does something have to be wrong for me to come see you?"

"Because I know you. I'm your momma."

"Okay, you got me."

"I know, so go ahead and spit it out. Tell momma what's wrong."

"I'm pregnant again, mom."

"Sweetheart, you ought to be happy. You got your husband back and now you're going to be growing your family so why do you look sad."

With tears welling up in her eyes Kyla says, "I don't think Vince and I are going to make it."

"He isn't happy about the baby?"

"No, that's not it. He's excited about the baby."

"Well then, I don't understand."

"He got another woman pregnant, mom," Kyla said, bursting into full tears.

"Oh, sweetheart. I'm sorry. When did this happen?" Mrs. Carter asked as she embraced her crying daughter.

"When we broke up."

"I know you're not going to want to hear this but sometimes karma catches up with you at the worst of times. I tell you girl, the universe has a funny sense of humor."

"What's funny about this?"

"That you would be sitting here thinking about walking away from your husband for the very same thing he walked away from you for."

"It's not exactly the same though mom."

"Actually, yours might have been worse. At least you weren't together when he started seeing another woman."

"Mom, you are supposed to be on my side."

"No, I supposed to be on the side of what's right and what you did was wrong and you are lucky that he forgave you because most men wouldn't have."

"So you're saying that I should forgive him for this."

"I'm not telling you what to do because you have to do what feels right for you. It's your marriage. But I am saying that you should think before you act. Finding out your husband is having a child with someone else is one of the toughest things that a woman has to deal with but you're strong."

"I don't know if I'm that strong."

"You are because I raised you to be. I've never told you or anyone else but your father had an affair when we were going through a rough patch early in our marriage. Your sister was just a baby and the woman he had an affair with came to my job and told me that she was pregnant by your father. I couldn't contain myself. I wanted to kill him but I knew I couldn't do that. I left work, marched home and confronted your father. He admitted to having a brief affair and that the woman was claiming to be pregnant by him after he broke it off with her. I was prepared to pack up and move but I realized that I had a young family and I wasn't about to let this woman ruin that. I stayed but it was hard to think about how our lives would be changed by a baby that wasn't ours together."

"So dad has another child out here?"

"Not that I know of because after your dad got a hold of her for coming to my job, she packed up and moved. We never heard from her again and don't even know if she was really pregnant because back then, you didn't get little pictures of the baby to take home from the doctor's office on the spot like you all do now. If she had the baby, she never told him and raised it alone."

"That's deep, mom. You really are a strong woman, you know that."

"And so are you."

"There is one other problem that makes all of this very complicated."

"What's that?"

"I know this woman very well."

197

"Who is she?"

"Sal's sister."

Mrs. Carter was speechless for a moment and then she said, "Of all of the women in Philadelphia, how did he manage to find that boy's sister and get her pregnant?"

"They met at Melanie's daycare and he didn't know she was related to Sal."

"What on earth was she doing at the daycare?"

"Sal's son Aaron goes there too."

"Well cut my legs off and call me shorty," her mom said jokingly.

"Come on mom, this isn't funny."

"I know it isn't but I'm stunned."

"Just tell me what I should do. Do you really think that we can survive this?"

"I'm not going to tell you what to do. Just follow your heart and it will lead you in the right direction."

"If I had followed my heart a long time ago I would have been married to Sal and not to Vince and we all wouldn't be stuck in this crazy situation."

"You wouldn't have been following your heart; you would have been following something else. I don't know that marrying Sal would have been the answer. You are with the man that you are supposed to be with."

"If that's the case then why does Sal keep finding a way to be a part of my life?"

"Because you keep letting him. He can't go where he isn't wanted. You have a good man in your life—one that I'm proud to call son-in-law. You are about to have two beautiful children together and that's no mistake."

"Mom, why do you always have to get so deep?"

"When you get my age, GOD gives you wisdom. I want you to go home and pray about this. Seriously seek GOD's counsel before you make any decisions. Babies are a gift from GOD and whether or not you like it, he is using that girl as a vessel. If you find that you truly will not be able to stay in the marriage, tell him sooner rather than later. No need in dragging it out and ruining a bunch of lives in the process. I love you, baby girl."

"I love you too, mom," Kyla said, before giving her mom a big hug before leaving the restaurant.

Kyla left the restaurant and went to the park to think and process all that her mother had just laid on her. She sat down on the bench, watched the kids playing and listened to nature. The fall leaves were an indication of change and the cold air told her that a wintery storm was coming that she needed help getting through. She closed her eyes and began to pray, following her mother's advice and seeking GOD's counsel. She began to ask GOD to show her what she should do. She asked him to point her in the right direction and to release her anger, bitterness, and resentment toward the innocent child that was going to be coming into this situation soon. She felt a release when she was done but she knew that she still had to wait on GOD's direction before making any lasting decisions. She collected herself after about an hour in the park and headed home. When she got there, Vince's car was in the driveway. She wasn't ready to see him yet; she was still angry with him and not ready to deal with her emotions. When she opened up the door she saw him standing right in front of her.

He pulled her into an embrace and said, "Kyla, I couldn't sleep last night thinking about losing you. You, Melanie, and now this new little one are my world. When I called you at work to check on you, Frank said that you weren't there so I got worried. I left work to come straight over here."

"I'm fine. I just needed some time to myself to think. I was ready to walk away and leave all this behind and just be happy raising our children together but I prayed about it and the fact that you're standing here means that GOD has spoken. I'm not sure what GOD is trying to tell me but I don't think he is through with us yet."

"What GOD has brought together, let no man put asunder," Vince said, as he leaned in to kiss Kyla on the lips and this time, she let him.

Epilogue

After a tumultuous year and a half of secrets and lies, of breakups and make-ups that threatened to derail her upwardly mobile career, Kyla was finally reaching new heights at work. She received a promotion to Equity Partner in her firm and it was time to celebrate with friends and family. Mrs. Carter was shutting down the restaurant on a Saturday evening to throw a big gathering in Kyla's honor. Kyla walked into the party feeling on top of the world. She had her husband, Vince, on her arm and her two children in tow. Melanie was the doting big sister to Layla, who was just three months old and the Preston's couldn't have asked for a better life right now. Things between Vince and her were going way better than expected with the help of Kyla's therapist, Dr. Ellis. They were trusting and loving one another again and ready for what life had to bring. Kyla was no longer angry about Vincent Jr., who was now seven months old. She was working on accepting him and being able to be in the same space with him and his mother. That was still a work in progress but, for now, they were all good.

As they celebrated Kyla and danced, toasted, and ate the night away they didn't have a care in the world—at least until Sal started calling Kyla at the end of the party. She ignored his calls and sent him to voicemail because there wasn't anything for them to talk about at this point in their lives. He wouldn't stop calling. She finally decided to excuse herself from her guests, step into the foyer, and answer the phone after the third time that he called.

"What do you want?" Kyla asked.

"Kyla, is Vince with you?" Sal asked.

"Yes he is, why?"

"He needs to get to the hospital."

"What's wrong?"

"Little Vince has stopped breathing and they rushed him to the hospital in an ambulance a little while ago. I'm on my way there now."

"Oh no. Let me get him. What hospital did they take him to?"

"He's at Children's Hospital."

"We'll be right there."

Kyla rushed back into the party and found Vince. He was talking to some of her colleagues before she frantically interrupted.

"What's the matter?" he asked, after seeing her in a panicked state.

"It's Vince Jr.," She said.

"What about him?"

"Sal called and said that he was rushed to Children's Hospital because he stopped breathing."

"Why didn't Annette call me?"

"I don't know? Check your phone."

"Shit! It's off. Let me get over there."

"I'm coming with you."

"No. You stay with the kids. I'll call you when I know something."

Vince rushed out of the party, jumped in his car and raced top speed from Northern Liberties to University City. He got there in record time. He ran from the parking garage up into the hospital and got stopped by security.

"Can I help you, sir?" the security guard asked.

"My son was brought here in an ambulance," Vince responded in a panic.

"See the receptionist over there to find out what room he's in."

"Thank you," Vince said, before going to the reception desk.

"How can I help you?" the receptionist asked.

"I'm looking for my son Vincent Preston Jr. He was brought in because he stopped breathing."

"He's in room 4."

"Thank you."

Vince made his way to room 4, where he saw Annette holding Vince Jr. and Sal sitting in the chair across from her. He was relieved to see that his son was actually breathing.

"What happened? Vince asked.

"He was crawling around on the floor and put something in his mouth and choked but I didn't know until he started turning blue. I called the ambulance and they came and dislodged the object but brought him

201

here to be checked out and make sure his airways are clear and he was getting enough oxygen to his brain," Annette said.

"Why weren't you watching him?"

"Look don't come in here judging her, it was an accident." Sal stood up and said.

"You need to sit down because this doesn't concern you. I'm talking to Annette about *my* son. Now again, why weren't you watching him?"

"I don't have to explain myself to you. You can go back to your happy family. Your perfect little wife. He's okay now."

"No, that's not how this works. If you're not going to be a responsible parent, I might need to think about a custody agreement."

"You're not going to take my son from me."

"You need to get out of here with that shit," Sal said.

"Again, you need to shut the fuck up," Vince said.

The nurse walking by could hear them arguing and it was getting very heated so she stepped into the room and said, "Gentleman, I'm going to have to ask you to keep it down or you will have to leave."

"I'm sorry," Sal said, as he flashed her a devilish grin and she smiled back.

"Don't think I'm playing with you Annette. I will be looking into custody options since you can't pay attention to my son," Vince said, as he bent down to take him from her.

"You're seriously over-reacting," she said, as she handed him to Vince.

Vince rocked him and played with him for about two hours until the nurse came in with the discharge papers.

"You are free to go. Remember to keep small objects away from the baby's reach. We wouldn't want him to choke on anything else. Babies are quick and if you look away for a second, a tragedy could strike. You got lucky this time. Take care," the nurse said, before leaving.

"See," Vince said.

"See what?" Annette asked.

"You have to pay attention to him at ALL times."

"You try being a single parent and see how it feels to have a baby stuck to you 24/7. You can't do anything in peace."

"You chose this life."

"With *your* help."

"I'm going to go now but I'll be by your house to check on him tomorrow."

"Goodbye, Vince."

"Goodbye," Vince said, before leaving the room.

Vince got back in his car and hurried home to Kyla and the girls. He was tired but all he could think about was the well-being of his son. He came in the house and headed upstairs, got undressed and slipped in the bed next to Kyla.

Half asleep she mumbles, "Is everything okay?"

"He's okay now but I I'm not," Vince replied.

Kyla sat up in the bed, turned on the night light and asked, "What's the matter?"

"I want custody of my son."

Kyla sat there stunned because she definitely wasn't ready for those words to come out of his mouth.

"You can't just take that woman's baby."

"He's my baby too and she isn't fit to care for him."

"You're basing this off of what exactly?"

"The fact that she let my son almost choke to death on a foreign object because she wasn't watching him."

"That is one incident and she wouldn't be the first parent to do that. I think you're over-reacting."

"That's one too many. She said it herself, she wasn't paying attention and he was a burden on her."

"She'll never let you take him without a fight."

"That's why I have you."

"You're going to need a lot more proof than this one incident to make her an unfit mom. Besides, have you even thought about what you're asking me to do? You are asking me to take on the responsibility of a THIRD child. One that isn't even mine. Hell, one that I barely can stomach now and he doesn't even come over here for a visit. Vince, I didn't sign up for that."

"I am thinking about what's best for my son right now. I'll worry about the logistics later."

"So that's it. You've made up your mind."

"Yes."

"Well, I can tell you now that I'm not going to be a part of this plan so good luck and I hope you find you a great family lawyer," Kyla said, as she cut out her light and rolled over to go back to sleep.

Vince just laid there in silence with nothing more to say because his mind was already made up.